Southerly Wind

Gold Brooch

FRID INGULSTAD

Translated from Norwegian by Wyonne Long
with Frid Ingulstad

Published by BookLocker.com, Inc., Bradenton, Florida.

The characters and events in this book are fictitious. Any similarity to real persons, living or dead is coincidental and not intended by the author.

Cover Illustration: Erlend Tønnesen
Photographer: Bård Ek
History Consultant: Øystein Eike
Translation: Wyonne Long

Printed in the United States of America on acid-free paper.

BookLocker.com, Inc.
2013

Visit the author's website: www.ingulstad.no
Write to the author: frid@ingulstad.no
Write to the agent/translator: wyonne@hotmail.com

Register of Persons

Elise Løvlien – 18 years old. Lives in Sandakerveien in Sagene, a section of Kristiania, Norway. Works as a spinning girl at Nedre Vøien Spinderi, must be "mother" for her siblings.

Hilda – Her sister, 16 years old. Works as bobbin girl at the same spinning mill as Elise.

Kristian – Their brother, 9 years old. Different personality, hard and reserved.

Peder – Their "little brother," 8 years old. Thin, scrawny and has sensitive feelings.

Jensine Løvlien – Their mother, in late 30's. Confined to bed with tuberculosis, moved to Kristiania from a working class family at Ulefoss, in Telemark region of Norway. Concerned with integrity and righteousness. Religious.

Mathias Løvlien – Their father. Was sailor in merchant marine, an alcoholic. Has *tater* (gypsy) blood in his veins.

Johan Thoresen – Elise's childhood friend and sweetheart, lives one floor below in Andersensgården tenement building.

Anna Thoresen – Johan's sister, has polio, lame and bedridden at home.

Fru Thoresen (Aslaug) – Johan and Anna's mother, works at Hjula Veveri.

Evert – Orphan, 8 years old. Placed by the Poorhouse to live with Hermansen, an alcoholic. The Poorhouse pays Hermansen.

Emanuel Ringstad – Soldier in the Salvation Army, 27 years old. Only child and *odelsgutt* to Ringstad *gård*. Rents an attic room from Oscar Carlsen. (See glossary)

Herr Paulsen – *Verksmester* at Nedre Vøien Spinderi. Middle–aged, fat widower, no children, gets Hilda pregnant. Lives in Akersbakken, an upper–class section of Kristiana.

Agnes Zakariassen – Girlfriend of Elise. Lives with parents in Maridalsveien. Works at Hjula Veveri.

Fru Evertsen – One of the "street gossipers." Lives on first floor in Andersengården tenement building.

Valborg – Friend of Hilda. Nosey busy-body. Works at Nedre Vøien Spinderi.

Maren Sørby – Captain and slum-sister in the Salvation Army.

Oline – Widow with 4 children. Spinner at Nedre Vøien Spinderi. Was fired.

Magna on the Corner – Owner of small corner grocery store.

Turd-Anders – Acquaintance of Johan when they were sailors. Doubtful character, criminal.

Forward

There isn't any other capitol city in the world that has a river with so many waterfalls running through the city. That river is Akerselva and today the river and surrounding parks are rightfully preserved and protected cultural areas with many beautiful and romantic walking trails, but how was it along the river over one hundred years ago?

How was it be to a factory girl working at Nedre Vøien Spinderi in 1905 and stand 12–14 hours a day in a factory hall filled with dust and ear deafening noises from all the machines? How was it to live 10–12 people in one small room and kitchen, and how did a mother feel leaving her flock of young children home alone when she was forced to be away at work, in a time when they only had kerosene lamps, candlelight and heated with wood?

In the *Southerly Wind* series, we follow eighteen year old Elise in her misery and happiness, in her romance, her struggle to survive and her responsibility for her younger siblings.

The people are fictional, but the circumstances are built around facts. I have used the area and buildings where I've been many times myself and I've used references and information that older folks have given me. I have interviewed elderly descendants who are still living in the area; they are calling me wanting to share their memories of that time. They are folks whose families worked in the factories and lived in the area at the time. Some of them still exist. It was a hard life, totally different from ours, but they also had lighter sides. They had the ability to be happy with small things, and romance was the same at that time as now.

Frid Ingulstad

(PS: Frid leads tours through the area annually – each time there are as many as 600-700 readers who are eager to see where Elise and her family lived and worked.)

Chapter 1

Kristiania, Early January, 1905

"Get out of here right now! I don't care if all your kids got the measles. That ain't my problem." The foreman's right hand shot out pointing toward the door and his sharp, thundering voice was heard everywhere in the factory.

Elise stopped suddenly, scared, as she glanced over to the next room. Who was getting it this time? She shuddered, stood still and listened. Who was the poor soul whose children were all sick? She had heard the measles epidemic was spreading like wildfire over all of Sagene, and half of those who'd caught the measles had already died.

The foreman continued his rage, "Go to the office! Get your pay and don't think for a minute you can work here anymore! What would happen to the spinning mill if all the workers just showed up when they felt like it?" His voice got louder and sharper. Elise was suffering along with the poor soul who was the object of his wrath, but she couldn't see who it was. Should she sneak a few steps nearer and try to peek in?

She tip-toed quietly a bit closer and stretched to see. She had to know who it was. The foreman stood in the middle of the room, his face red as a lobster, his double chin quivering, a furious look in his eyes. Oline stood, with her back to Elise, head bowed, in front of him. Her fragile arms were tightly folded around her thin, sunken body as she stared at the floor, trembling trying to hold back the tears.

"It's the second time this week you're late and that's it! Get out! I won't have anything to do with such good-for-nothin's."

Elise watched with increasing fright. Oline was a widow, the mother of four small children. If she lost her job, there would be no income, no money. They'd starve.

Elise held her breath when Oline dropped to her knees, pulling on the foreman's pant-legs, begging tearfully, "Please, I promise it'll never happen again. My little boy was delirious with fever and acting so strange. I thought he was going to die in my arms."

Furious, the foreman shoved her away, "Get out of here I said. It's not my fault you've brought so many kids into the world!"

Oline struggled to stand upright, turned and stumbled tearfully towards the door. Elise quickly moved back and pretended to be putting her shawl on when Oline came out. Inside, Elise was seething with a fury that almost took her breath away. Enraged, she thought how unfair it was. One day...one day he will suffer... She clenched her fists in anger.

Oline didn't look at her, but with tears in her eyes, her feet unsteady, she went to the office to get her pay. Elise wasn't sure Oline even saw her. Elise pulled her coarsely knit shawl tightly around her shoulders and pushed open the heavy factory door. Her only thoughts were about Oline's awful situation. There would be no way out for Oline but the poorhouse. How could she and her four children live on so little? Was it so strange that she couldn't leave her sick little boy? She had no one to care for the children, and now they were all sick.

Elise was hit by icy-cold, heavy snow flakes swirling through the air. She shivered and bent her head into the fierce wind. The winter cold was even worse when she was so thin. Her boots were worn through, the soles coming off. She hadn't trudged very far before the slush pushed in and froze her toes. Before she got home she would have frostbite, just as she'd had yesterday.

Elise thought about the daughter of the director. She had come waltzing into the factory, wearing a new warm winter coat, fur-trimmed, with matching fur cap and muff, and new, warm lace-up boots. She didn't suffer in the cold with a blue nose or red cheeks. She laughed and joked with the *verksmester* and didn't seem to have a care in the world.

But then she wasn't a factory worker, tied to a spinning machine until her dying day. Elise sighed. *She* didn't have to work from six o'clock in the morning until six or eight o'clock at night, with the ear-splitting noises from the machinery, drive shafts on the ceiling and hundreds of bobbins spinning around and around making you dizzy, a thick fog of swirling dust that clogged your mouth and nose, plus straining your eyes to make sure that threads didn't break. She didn't have to hurry home to a sick mother, two noisy little brothers, a younger sister worn out from a long day at her job as a bobbin girl at the spinning mill, and a father who squandered his wages for something far different than he should. The director's daughter sat in her warm living room, waited on by the parlor maid. She had fine clothes and dry feet, ate as much as she liked, and went to bed when she felt like it. It must be heavenly to live like that!

Secretly, Elise and her friend Agnes snickered at the director. He was short with a big pot-belly and looked unbelievably comical as he swayed through the factory each morning, smacking his pale lips in disapproval.

Doubled up against the sharp wind, Elise hurried over Beierbrua, the bridge they crossed over every day. It was unusual for the wind to be so sharp and strong this time of year, just after Christmas. Her worn and wet stockings rubbed against the inside of her boots, and she could feel new holes in the heels that hadn`t been there this morning. She would have to darn her stockings again tonight. But poor Oline! What would happen to her? It had been hard before, and now it would be even worse.

Both the spinning and weaving mills had midday hour-long breaks, from twelve to one o'clock, and she had to hurry to the store on the corner and pick up a few things: milk, soap, coffee, coal for the stove, and kerosene for the lamps. They still had gas lighting on Sandakerveien, but on the other side of the river they had gotten electric lights. Agnes had told her that the director's home on Oscarsgate had electric lights in all the rooms. That must be like a castle in a fairy tale, imagine just turning a switch!

Fortunately she had cooked potatoes last night so she could just heat them up again. This morning before work she had gone down and gotten water from the pump on the corner, where all the women got their water. If she hurried, she would make it before she had to go back to work. She swung around the corner to hurry into the store, relieved to get away from the icy snow, when she saw Evert, her little brother Peder's best friend. He was struggling trying to push a cart full of things to sell. She stopped in surprise. "Aren't you in school today, Evert?"

Evert shook his head and was about to hurry on.

"Why not?"

"They won't let me." His voice was surly, as if there was something he didn't want to talk about. "The poorhouse said no," he shouted as he disappeared around the corner.

Elise stood still for a moment. Evert wasn't allowed to continue in school even though he was one of the smartest in the class. It was terribly unfair. Evert was an orphan and a pauper and had been placed with Hermansen, a derelict, who got money from the poorhouse to take care of him.

Hermansen drank up both his wages and the money from the poorhouse so Evert was always hungry. Peder had told Elise he often shared his lunch pack with Evert. He would sneak a piece of bread into Evert's desk when no one was looking. Sometimes Evert would fall asleep in class because he had been working all night at the factory. Peder said when this happened, the teacher would get angry and pull his ear until it bled and almost fell off. Again Elise felt furious, and tramped angrily into the store.

A short time later, hurrying into the backyard at home, she was met with the horrid stench from the outhouse. The garbage cans were overflowing, oozing out from under the lids, more trash and junk heaped beside them. A rat scurried under the neighboring fence, but he would certainly be back when the yard was quiet again. She hurried in the door and up the stairs to the third floor.

It was cold in the kitchen. Before checking on her mother in the *kammers,* she fired up the wood stove, wondering why Hilda wasn't home yet. She had caught a glimpse of her before she left the factory, but hadn't taken the time to wait for her. She ladled water into a kettle, careful not to rattle the iron rings on the woodstove as she drew them aside. She put the kettle over the fire, and then cracked the door to the *kammers*.

Her mother lay with closed eyes, hands folded over the blanket, the way she usually laid every day.

"Mamma?" she said softly. She didn't want to wake her, but had to be sure she was still alive. Her mother's eyes flickered open, and she gave a faint smile.

"There you are," she said in a weak voice and closed her eyes again.

Elise went quietly back to the kitchen. There were only the two rooms in the small apartment, but she was grateful at least they did not have to share it with another family as so many people had to. She wiped the table with a cloth, and set out the tin plates, knives and mugs. Hilda would surely be here soon.

Elise thought the noon hour was the best part of the day. It was a blessing to get away from the noise and dust at the spinning mill, and it helped her aching back to move around. With her brothers at school and Mamma in bed, she and Hilda were alone.

Hilda was sixteen, two years younger than she, with blond hair, freckles, an upturned nose and deep dimples. They looked a lot alike, but Elise had brown hair. Despite their age difference, they snickered and laughed at the same things, told each other secrets, and gossiped a little about the other girls at the spinning mill.

Of course they missed having their mother there. Before she got sick, she came home at noon, too, and they all three ate together. When Pappa was still working, he sometimes ate with them, too, but that was a long time ago. Nowadays he spent most of his time with his drinking cronies. She shook away thoughts of Pappa.

Elise heard steps in the stairwell and soon Hilda came in.

Elise turned to her. Her sister had become pale and thin lately. Maybe she'd gotten tuberculosis, too, Elise thought frantically. Was it any wonder that people got sick when they had to work from morning until night in all the noise and dust? She remembered what Mamma had said once, that there wouldn't be any real revolt against all the injustice until Norway became independent. Now there were rumors circulating that the union between Norway and Sweden would soon be dissolved. The father of Agnes, Elise's best friend, followed the news. Agnes was an only child and her father told her what he knew. Agnes talked about it with Elise so she, too, knew a little about their country's politics. She wondered if it would help if Norway got its independence, but doubted it would make much difference since those in power paid more attention to the rich than to those who had nothing.

"You aren't sick, are you, Hilda?" She looked at Hilda's pale face.

Hilda shook her head. "I'm freezing all the time. And I'm dizzy from all the noise. Agnes says we'll lose our hearing eventually. Several have already. We walked home together. She thought I looked terrible, too."

"Warm up by the stove, I'll hurry and get the food ready."

If Hilda gets sick, I don't know what I'll do, Elise thought. With Mamma sick in bed, Pappa hanging around in beer-joints, and Peder and Kristian in school, she wouldn't be able to make ends meet on her wages. She only made seven kroner ($1.90) per week, and it all went to food, rent and fuel. Eighty øre ($.23) for bread, syrup and coffee for breakfast, fifty-seven øre ($.18) for fish, potatoes and carrots for dinner, fifty øre ($.15) for milk, bread, butter and coffee for Saturday and Sunday dinners, twenty-five øre ($.07) for oatmeal for the evening meal, three kroner and fifty øre ($.95) for rent and one krone fifty øre ($.41) for candles and fuel. Hilda had to give her the money she earned so they would have some money for clothes, shoes, soap, a newspaper now and then, and all the other stuff they needed. And she did, mostly without protesting, but still nothing was left over.

Last week she had to borrow almost half the rent money from Johan. She had no idea where he got the money, but he was as kind as the day was long and never refused when she asked him for something. She hated to ask for help. Life wasn't easy for Johan, either, with his father at sea, his mother working at the spinning mill and a sister crippled from polio. "She will never be well," Johan had said sadly.

Johan had also lived in the Andersengården tenement building since he was little. When they were small he had been her only playmate, and when the other children teased her about her freckles and pug nose, he had always defended her and threatened to beat them up. Johan was the biggest and strongest of all the boys in Sagene and something else about him inspired respect. Even the teacher treated him differently than the other pupils, maybe because Johan had taught himself to speak more "properly" than the other kids in the street. Elise's mother always said Johan had been born a grown-up. From the time he was a little boy of four or five, he had opened doors for all the women in the building, bowed politely, and asked if he could help them with anything.

Special warmth spread through Elise when she thought about Johan. They had become sweethearts last summer. Even though she had thought of him as a kind of big brother from the time she was little, suddenly something happened between them. It was on a Sunday, when they were on their way home from a meeting at the Salvation Army. Both their mothers attended the meetings there, and the kids had gone along, at least in earlier years. Now they didn't have time as often, or, if she was honest, she had to admit they would rather be doing something else . . . She smiled remembering the sidewalk was slick and slippery after all the rain that day. She slipped and would have fallen if he hadn't caught her. But instead of letting her go when she regained her balance, he stood holding her. Before she realized it, she felt his mouth on hers, two warm soft lips against her own. It was her first kiss! She had imagined it would be repulsive, an older girlfriend had told her that once, but then bragged about all those who wanted to kiss her and touch her. To Elise's astonishment, it felt good. Very good!!

There had been many kisses since that day. . .

She knew several of the girls at the spinning mill envied her. Some of them taunted her and wondered what Johan could see in a scrawny girl with freckles and a pug nose. She had gone into the *kammers*, looked at herself in the little mirror on the wall and had to agree that her face was boring and dull, at least when she was serious. But when she smiled, her dimples showed and that helped!

She had seen a couple of the girls hanging around the backyard in the evenings, snickering and laughing in the dark while they looked up curiously at Johan's window. She could tell he knew they were there, but he acted as if he didn't. Once Elise had asked if he didn't feel a little arrogant when girls chased after him like that, but he shrugged his shoulders carelessly as if the other girls didn't interest him. That made her happy and confident, filled with quivering warmth.

"I ran into Johan when I was coming in," Hilda said suddenly, as if she had read Elise's thoughts. "It looked like he was waiting for you."

Elise hoped he didn't need the money he had lent her. The thought upset her. The tenement manager was merciless. If the rent wasn't paid on time, there was no grace period. She put the potatoes and fish on the table. They couldn't afford carrots today. "I saw Oline get fired today."

Hilda looked up with alarm. "She was fired?"

Elise pressed her lips tightly together. "She was late for the second time in a week."

"But all her kids have the measles."

"I know. The youngest was so sick she was afraid he was dying."

Hilda took only a small piece of fish and half a potato. "That was a horrible thing for The Frog to do." She was referring to the foreman. They called him The Frog because he sounded like a croaking frog when he got mad and all worked up. And that happened often.

Elise nodded with concern at her sister as her anxiety grew. "You're not eating much, are you okay?"

Hilda shook her head, "I just feel so strange."

"In what way?"

"My ears are ringing, and sometimes I feel a little shaky."

Elise didn't say anything for a while, but then she said, "See if you can't eat something anyway. That will help."

Hilda forced herself to eat another bite, then gave up and put her fork down. "You can have the rest."

Elise eagerly ate every bite, nothing would go to waste. "Go in to Mamma and tell her how you're feeling. Maybe she will know what it is. And ask her if she would like something to eat."

Hilda did as she was told, but when she came back, she seemed even more exhausted. She was so cold her teeth were chattering. "Mamma was tired and didn't say much, but she mumbled something about the flu. She didn't want anything to eat."

"If you can't go back to work, I'll let them know."

Hilda shook her head firmly. "Do you really think The Frog will tolerate my staying home? When he fired Oline for being late twice?"

Elise didn't say anything. She knew that Hilda was right. The foreman didn't put up with anyone staying home just because of a fever or a cough, no matter how bad it was. Many had been fired for less.

As soon as Hilda left, Elise quickly poured hot water from the kettle into the dishpan and washed the two tin plates, cups, knives and forks. The wind was howling in the stovepipe, it must be even stronger now, and she dreaded going out. When she finished she left the soapy water in the dishpan; it was too good to throw out. She would scrub the floor when she came home again.

Out on the sidewalk, Elise almost lost her breath from the blasting wind. It cut through her clothes, stung her face and burned her ears. She bent over, wrapping her arms in her coarse-knit shawl and holding it tightly around her body.

Then suddenly she noticed something shiny amidst the broken twigs and old leaves swirling between clumps of snow. Could it be a coin? She bent down and snatched up the shiny object. She stood starring at what was laying in her hand. It was not money - not a five kroner coin, or even a one krone coin. It was something completely different, something she had never before seen close-up, and certainly never held in her hand. It was a glittering piece of jewelry, a beautiful gold brooch set with small sparkling stones.

Elise held her breath. Who could have lost such a valuable piece of jewelry? She looked around, searching. There was no one in sight. No one from around here could have lost such a valuable brooch, no one from Sagene. And nobody who lived along Akerselva.

There was only one person she could imagine owning such a valuable brooch, the director's daughter, but she was never in this area. Whenever she visited her father at the factory, she always arrived in a horse-drawn carriage. The director had even bought an automobile that could move without a horse pulling it. Johan told her the horse-drawn carriage drivers were furious. It had been bad enough when the electric trolleys replaced the horse drawn trolley cars fifteen years ago. The trolley horses had been so frightened by the noisy spectacles rolling through the streets that someone suggested placing a stuffed horse at the front of all the electric trolleys to calm the horses.

Elise glanced around again, and then hurriedly dropped the glittering brooch in her apron pocket. It felt as if it was burning - like a hot lead weight. Her heart raced. This is what a thief feels like, she thought suddenly. If the brooch was discovered, they would think she had stolen it. She would be sent to prison with a long, stiff sentence. No one would believe she had found it. The story was much too unbelievable! She couldn't tell Mamma. She was much too sick to worry about this. She couldn't tell Pappa. He would take it from her, sell it and drink away the money, as he did with everything he got his hands on. She didn't even dare tell her best friend, Agnes, though they shared all their secrets. Agnes would surely tell her father, and he too would think she had stolen it. No, the only person she could tell was Johan. She couldn't talk to him until late tonight, but he would know what to do.

Anxiety nearly strangled her, she gasped for air! Why had she been the unlucky one to find the brooch? And why had she been dumb enough to pick it up? She should have left it there.

Chapter 2

Would this day never end? The hours were creeping along at a snail's pace.

As Elise looked around the spinning mill hall she understood that all were shocked that Oline had been fired. The gray, exhausted, worn out faces were even more bitter than usual. She tried to concentrate on her work, but her mind was filled with thoughts of Oline and the unfairness of her terrible fate, and of the costly brooch in her apron pocket.

The Frog was louder than usual, his voice even drowned out the noise from the nearby rushing waterfalls and the pounding spinning machines. He was never satisfied, barking orders and scolding workers. The bobbin girls ran back and forth like crazy with new bobbins. Huge drive shafts were turning around and around, the spinner girls screaming and hollering for new bobbins, and the bobbin girls ran even faster. The spinner girls did piece-work, and constantly shouted at the bobbin girls if they weren't fast enough.

Hilda worked in the other end of the huge factory hall. Elise worried about her. She knew Hilda couldn't hurry if she didn't feel good. There had been many a time when Elise had gone to work, her whole body aching, and coughing so hard she could hardly breathe. It was Hilda's turn now.

If one of the bobbin girls dared to take even a little breather, The Frog was there immediately, angry as all get out. "Ten-*øre* fine for wasting time," he demanded.

Ten *øre* ($.03) – more than an entire hour's wages, Elise thought.

Today the only thing that could help Hilda, who was a bobbin girl, would be if threads broke and the spinning machine had to be stopped.

In the next moment her thoughts returned to the strange object in her pocket. She could stop working, go to the office and show the director and tell him where she had found it. The thought occurred to her several times, but each time she was ready to go she lost her confidence. Imagine if he refused to believe she had found it on the sidewalk, a street where his daughter or others with beautiful jewelry would never set foot. Maybe it didn't belong to his daughter at all, and he would be even more suspicious. The thought made her sick.

She tried to force herself to think of something else. First her thoughts went back to Oline and her four small children, and she wondered how it was going with the boy in a feverish coma and "suddenly became so strange." She could feel the rage rising again. It was so unfair to fire Oline when she was late because her youngest child was deathly ill. She could feel herself boiling. She hoped The Frog would one day suffer as well.

Her thoughts went to how strange it would be if Norway became a separate country, governing itself, no longer dependent on another nation, and with its own king. She was sure they'd get their very own king. Everyone said so. She thought about all the songs she had learned in school that told about Norway being a special country, different from others, songs like: *The Majestic Old Mountains*, written by Ivar Aasen, the father of the "new" Norwegian language. And she loved singing *There Lies a Land in Eternal Snow* written by Bjørnstjerne Bjørnson. He had also written Norway's national anthem. For the last day of school she had memorized the poem *Terje Vigen*, written by Henrik Ibsen, and it had made an impact on her. Five years ago the Norwegian flag – not the

"herring salad" flag with a small Swedish flag in the corner –
but a true Norwegian flag had flown proudly over the
Stortinget for the very first time, Agnes's father had told
them.

Her hand slid down into her pocket again. She hoped the
brooch wasn't made of real gold. Maybe it was just a cheap
imitation, and the shiny stones were made of glass. Then
nobody would suspect her of stealing. Many people bought
fake jewelry, and some even said it was hard for an untrained
eye to see the difference.

Johan had to help her with this. He was so smart and
wise and always knew a way. Maybe he would be kind
enough to bring it to the director for her. Maybe even run
down to the police station with it. She felt relieved at the
thought. Next time old Fru Berg offered her a piece of rock
candy she would hide it and give it to Johan. He deserved it.

Mamma had said Johan would go far in life because he
had such good manners, was good in school and never got
into any trouble. He should really still be in school, but since
they'd heard nothing from his father in a long time, and he
didn't send any money, they couldn't make it on what his
mother earned at the spinning mill, especially since his
paralyzed sister needed medicines and care. So Johan had to
continue working at the factory a while longer. Once he had
jokingly said he would do just like Rat-Anders. Rat-Anders
couldn't read or write, but he was smart. He had placed a
huge rat in a cage on the counter in his general store. The
factory workers flocked in to see the rat, and at the same time
bought things. That's the way Rat-Anders became rich.

Johan had a better head on his shoulders than most. Elise
was sure he would get a better paying job eventually, but that
wasn't the reason she was in love with him. She looked up to
him because he was so mature, so sure of himself. And he

was good looking, had beautiful eyes and was very kind to his mother and sister.

No, she was sure she would never find a better man than Johan, but, it was still too early to think about marriage. First they had to try to save some money and put it away in the bottom of the "hope chest." Nor did they have anywhere to live. It was too small and crowded to live with her family, but Johan said they'd eventually find a solution. Elise didn't know how, at least not as long as Peder and Kristian were going to school, but she trusted Johan. He would find a way. Maybe he had already saved some money.

Just last winter Mamma had wistfully said she wished they would end up together. Elise had only laughed. "Get married to Johan? You can't marry your big brother."

"What kind of nonsense is that?" Mamma had asked in a serious voice. Elise had quickly explained that she considered Johan more as a big brother because she had known him so long.

Last spring, however, she began to think differently about him. First she noticed she felt shy around him. At the same time she noticed he was different. She couldn't explain it, but she'd experienced it like a kind of sorrow. Something told her Johan was about to grow away from her. While she was still a young girl, he was developing into a mature man.

And then – this last summer – he kissed her. She smiled at the thought and was filled with a warm glow.

She glanced over at the huge windows. It had been dark for a long time now. Would this day never end?

She noticed Valborg, the nosey busy-body, looking at her curiously. She knew she had to pull herself together. If the director's daughter had lost the brooch and everyone at the spinning mill was interrogated, Valborg could very well mention that Elise had seemed scared and nervous, as if she had a guilty conscience. That could be disastrous.

Her thoughts returned to her sister, and she was overcome with worry. Hilda had not been herself lately. Not only pale and exhausted, she had been acting strangely. More serious and quiet, with her eyes turned inwards, as if struggling with something she didn't want to talk about. Elise had heard her crying one night, but when she had asked about it the next morning, Hilda had quickly looked away. Surprised at Hilda's reaction, Elise gradually realized the crying didn't come from a bad dream. She had been awake.

Why was she crying, and why wouldn't she tell Elisa? Nothing was different in their lives than before. Pappa had been drinking steadily over the past two years, and Mamma had been sick all this year. The factory hadn't changed, and even if they fell into bed every night dead-tired, it wasn't any worse than last year. Rather it was a little better since Hilda was a year older and was more used to the hard work.

Could Hilda be suffering from a broken heart? Elsie had gotten a glimpse of her over in Seilduksgate where she was standing with Lorang, the errand boy, laughing and joking. She had been happy when she came home afterwards. Lorang had seemed just as interested as Hilda, and that couldn't be anything to cry about. She should be happy – not sad.

Elise shuddered. Deep down a fear lurked, a thought she still hadn't dared to let come to the surface. Whenever she wanted to do something about it, her courage weakened and she shoved it away. And now when she tried to ignore the brooch in her pocket, that secret thought edged its way in.

Something was happening with Hilda…something awful. Something that hurt too much to share with others. They had always trusted each other with everything.

It had been quite a while since she first noticed it. Hilda had been down in the backyard, and when she came up, there were droplets of sweat on her forehead, even though it had been freezing cold. She looked dazed; her eyes were huge and scared. "What's going on with you?" Elise had asked, but Hilda was fidgety and had turned abruptly and started clattering with the iron rings on the cook stove to set over the coffee pot – even though the coffee was still hot.

There was something else, too. She and Hilda used to have their "monthly" at the same time. They had taken turns washing the disgusting, crocheted pads. But it had been a long time since Hilda had put any in the zinc bucket to soak......

Hilda was only sixteen... Their mother would surely die from this and their father would lose his mind, yelling and screaming, maybe even beat them all half to death if he was in that mood. And how could they feed one more? Elise's wages would be all they had to live on.

The thread broke; she stopped the machine and spliced the threads. Then she sat on the box and waited for the wheels to start turning again.

Could Hilda really have been so dumb? Of course, she wasn't the only one. Screaming kids were all over the place. Even the unmarried factory girls had them. One baby after another was turned in at The Crib before the factory sirens howled early in the morning, and they were all picked up again by their mothers, late at night. Elise had no idea how much they had to pay to keep the kids there all day, but it cost money, and she couldn't understand how they had money left over when the rent, food and coal for the stove were paid for. The kids sometimes cried and screamed keeping them up all night, but at six o'clock sharp the factory sirens demanded they come to work, sleep or no sleep. It was no life for someone with hardly any strength from before.

She shook her head and sighed. It hadn't been easy for her and Johan either. At least not last summer, when the ground was warmed by the sun, and Sunday went on for hours - long and glorious hours. They had walked to Nydalen, past the fields, between the trees. In a shady grove they had laid down together on the moss, stroked and touched each other with not a care in the world, wanting, needing, and burning with insatiable desire. They had kissed until they could no longer breathe.

She had managed to stop Johan whenever he became too eager...

Now had Hilda gone and gotten herself in trouble? With Lorang, the errand boy no less, who didn't make enough money for an extra crumb of bread. Oh Lord, what could be worse?!

The bobbin was empty, and she exchanged it with a full one with experienced fingers. Finally, the factory sirens! Elise sighed again. And in minutes she raced out with all the others.

The wind had died down, but the snow was still coming down - hard and heavy. Elise stuck her hand in her pocket to see if the brooch was still there. She was sort of hoping it had fallen out so it was no longer her problem.

At the same time she couldn't help thinking about how this precious object could rescue them - if it was real, of course - Mamma, Hilda, her brothers and herself. If she couldn't find the owner, the brooch belonged to her, didn't it? Then she could go to the pawnbroker, maybe get a few hundred *kroner* for it, enough for food and rent for several months. The thought made her dizzy.

Would God judge her if she kept it? She hadn't stolen it. It had just been laying there, as if it was meant for her to find it.

Of course she had to ask Johan. She had already decided as much, and she was sure he would say they first would try to find the owner.

But what if...?

Johan was mature, smart and sensible. And as Mamma had said, he was a good man. Honest. He would never do anything against the law. No, he would do what he could to find the owner. First he would ask The Frog and the office workers. Then he would build up his courage and go to the director or to the police.

But if none of them knew who owned the brooch, what would The Frog and the office workers do then? Take the brooch and keep it in the office until a possible owner showed up one day? Maybe she who owned the brooch had several and didn't even realize she had lost it? Then wouldn't God understand it was better to help Hilda, Mamma and her brothers than a person who had too much already? If there was any justice in this world...

Johan used to laugh at her when she talked about justice. "There is none," he had said. At least not in this lifetime and he wasn't so sure there was any in the next either. If there was justice, why didn't God fix it right away? Why wait until they left this earth?

But, just the same Elise had a vague perception that there was justice, even if she'd not seen much of it. What had happened to Oline today didn't give any hope for justice, though. When Elise was little, she had thought if you suffered as a child, you would have a good life when you got old, and those who got what they wanted growing up, would pay for it later.

Now she wasn't so sure. When she looked at the workers in the weaving and spinning mills there were plenty who had been standing in front of the machines since they were little girls, and were now bent over, wrinkled and gray. They hadn't been anywhere else but the cramped and crowded *kammers* at home and the factory before they got carted away in the *likkjerra* to Nordre Gravlund. Still, she refused to believe that she herself would be standing by the machine for the rest of her life. At least not if she married Johan.

"What's going on with you, Elise?"

Elise turned toward the voice behind her. It was Valborg. "What's going on with me? What do you mean? I'm like I always am."

Valborg cackled that nasty laughter Elise couldn't stand. "You're not kiddin' me none. Ever since you came back after lunch break, you've been completely out of it. You don't have to be so uptight and always keep everythin' to yourself!"

Elise was startled. What did Valborg mean by uptight? Did she know something? Had she seen her pick something off the ground? "I don't know what you mean. I'm the same as always. Except I'm mad at The Frog for firing Oline."

"Humph. *That* ain't what I meant." Valborg marched past her, nose in the air.

Elise followed her with her eyes until she disappeared in the snowy weather. She was nearly paralyzed with fear. She told herself Valborg only said that because she'd noticed Elise was nervous, but that didn't help. Valborg could have seen her, inspite of having turned and looked in all directions when she realized what she had found. Probably she hadn't been careful enough. Valborg could have come around the corner exactly when she put the brooch in her pocket. She could have seen it was something shiny.

As she started to walk across the bridge, she looked for Hilda but didn't see her. It wasn't easy to see anyone in the snow. Ahead she could barely make out some dark shadows, hurrying, bent against the snow, in the direction of the large tenement buildings. Their *skauts* were pulled all the way down on their foreheads and their shawls wrapped tightly around their skinny bodies. They're like black ants, she thought. Always moving, always hurrying from one place to another, with the huge, dark factory "ant-hill" as the gathering point. One of many "ant-hills," all with sirens that sounded off when you were barely awake and didn't sound off again until your body was heavy with fatigue.

This is how life is, she thought with a heavy sigh. Sleep, *kaffeskvett,* a bite of bread, and an endless day at the factory with all the noisy machines, then more coffee, another piece of bread and back to bed again. The only break was lunch hour, the only bright spot in a grey and dreary day. No, this wasn't what she wanted. She didn't run down to the tavern every Saturday and Sunday like so many others and spend the few *øre* she had managed to save.

"It's the only fun we have," was their excuse, but they forgot that the "only fun" stole away their chances for a better life.

Still, it wasn't right to judge them. They didn't have many chances for a better life, regardless of what they did. Not everyone had a man like Johan to help, with his strong hands, a good head on his shoulders and a strong will to succeed.

She saw the dark shadows ahead disappear into one dark backyard after another, and was happy none stopped and looked back. She wasn't in the mood to chat with anyone today. She couldn't concentrate on anything other than the brooch in her pocket and Hilda's misery.

Long before she came up to the third floor, she heard Peder and Kristian scuffling in the kitchen. Couldn't they get rid of some of that energy outside instead of making so much noise inside? She hurried up the steps and rushed in.

"Shhhh, boys. Haven't I told you to be quiet for Mamma?"

Peder and Kristian stopped immediately and looked at her guiltily. Kristian went straight to the table and pulled out his school lessons, but Peder, the meeker of the two, came over to her. "Don't be mad, Elise, it's only playin'." He pleaded with his huge, blue eyes and she melted immediately. She caringly brushed her fingers through his hair. "Have you seen Hilda?"

Peder shook his head. Then he grinned teasing. "No, but I seen someone else. Johan was just leavin' when we come home."

To her annoyance, Elise felt herself blush and turned away from him. "Have you been in to see Mamma?"

"Ja."

"How was she?"

"The same."

Elise went to the water bucket and filled a cup, then walked over to the *kammers* door and peeked in. The kerosene lamp was lit on the dresser. At least they had managed to light the lamp, even if they hadn't managed to stoke the fire, she sighed. It was really cold inside, even though she had stoked the fire well when she was home for lunch. The heat seemed to disappear through the thin walls.

Quietly, she walked to the bed. Mamma's head was turned away, her eyes half open, as if she was staring into another landscape, another world.

"Mamma, are you thirsty? Would you like something to drink?"

Mamma turned toward her, her skin tight and thin across high cheekbones, her brown hair swept away from her forehead and hanging in thin, scraggly strands against her head. Dear God, she hardly has any hair left, Elise thought and felt a lump in her throat. Mamma's eyes stared at her, the dark shadows underneath like craters now. She was surely marked by death, as Fru Evertsen, from the first floor, had said a few days ago when she had come up and looked in on them.

Elise held up the cup, and Mamma tried to lift her head from the pillow, but couldn't. Elise put the cup down and gently helped her into a sitting position, placed a couple pillows behind her and held her arm around her so she wouldn't fall backwards. Elise felt her ribs like sharp blades against her arm. Mamma tried to take a sip, but her dry, chapped lips stuck to the cup and she started to moan.

"Be careful, Mamma. I'll help you."

She gently lowered her mother onto the pillow, wet her fingers and managed to get Mamma's lips unstuck. She took the spoon from the dresser and forced a few drops of water into her dry mouth. She heard Mamma's difficulty in swallowing, like it was more than her worn out body could handle. Her chest rattled. She will start coughing soon, Elise thought, and then it would all come up again. She wiped Mamma's forehead with her rough sleeve. Fear clamped in Elise's chest.

"Where is Hilda?" Mamma's voice was merely a whisper. The words came in gasps.

"She's not back from the factory yet. I'm sure she's gossiping with some of the girls," she added quickly, not showing her increasing uneasiness. As miserable as she felt, Hilda should be hurrying home.

"And Peder and Kristian?" Mamma coughed, a few drops of water dribbled down her chin, like grey pearls. Elise wiped them away with the cloth folded on the dresser.

"They're in the kitchen, doing their school lessons. They came in and lit the lamp, but you were sleeping."

Mamma moved her hands and rested them on Elise's arm. Like pale yellow claws they lay on her sleeve. I have to cut her fingernails, Elise thought with concern.

Her mother's wide-open eyes rested on her, inquiringly. As if she wanted to say something, but couldn't.

"More water, Mamma?"

Her mother shook her head weakly. Then her eyes closed, and she fell into that heavy, cumbersome sleep that was her hiding place lately.

Elise moved her pillow to a better position so Mamma could sleep more comfortably. Straightened her aching back, she picked up the cup and cloth and left the *kammers* wondering if she would ever see her mother leave her bed.

She noticed Peder's worried facial expression, but he didn't say anything. For a while she didn't say anything, either. She couldn't lie to him; he understood the seriousness of the situation even if he was only eight years old.

"Where is Hilda?" Kristian asked without glancing up from his school lessons.

"She'll be here soon." Elise crumpled some pieces of old newspaper that were folded in a special way and had been innersoles in her boots. She put them in the stove, lay some kindling on top and got the fire going again.

"Evert says Hilda is running around on the other side of the bridge."

Elise turned toward him. "Running around on the other side of the bridge? What does he mean by that?"

Kristian shrugged his shoulders without looking at her. "I dun'no. That she's got somebody on the other side or somethin' like that."

Elise stood up quickly. "You're talking nonsense now!" She couldn't understand why all of a sudden she was so angry. "Don't just sit there and rattle on. Who do you mean?"

"I dun'no, I said. Evert says a lot of dumb things."

"Is he talking about Lorang, the errand boy?"

Kristian laughed. "Now what would he be doin' over there? Of course, you know who's on the west side of Akerselva."

"I don't know what you mean. If Hilda had been talking to any of *them* it had to be about work. Maybe she's been promoted from bobbin girl to spinner girl," she added, sounding hopeful.

Kristian didn't say more. As Elise made coffee and put some bread on the table for them, she tried to convince herself that could be the explanation.

At the same time, fantasies ran through her mind. Could it be possible she was meeting one of the office workers and not Lorang, the errand boy? Then it wouldn't be such a disaster. Even if the office workers were poor compared to the director, they earned far more money than the factory workers. Then maybe Mamma wouldn't be so upset even if Hilda was only sixteen.

Oh, stop it, she said to herself. She could have been imagining things. Both Hilda and she had been irregular many times before, especially when they were really worn out and hadn't eaten enough.

"Did you say Johan was on his way out, Peder?" She asked after a little while. "Where was he headed?"

"How would Peder know that?" Kristian said, annoyed.

Peder glanced at her with a glint in his eye. "Whad'a ya mean?"

"I only wanted to talk to him about something."

"Elise and Johan are sweethearts...Elsie and Johan are sweethearts..." Peder sang loudly, and Elise shushed him. "Not so loud! Mamma is sleeping. Here's your supper. Keep an eye on the stove while I run out real quick. I'll be back in a minute."

She grabbed her *skaut* and threw the shawl around her shoulders as she went out into the hallway.

She slowed down at the second floor. What if Johan told her to go to the factory and deliver the brooch immediately? Maybe he would get mad because she hadn't done it straight away. Maybe he would ask why she had kept it in her apron pocket all day. Johan was so sure of himself. He always knew what to do.

She knocked on the door and peeked inside. Fru Thoresen stood by the cook stove, with her back to the door. "Come in, Elise," she said without turning. She was cooking *grøt*, the room smelled of scalded milk.

"I was wondering if Johan was home."

"He left before I knew it. Come in and sit down. Tell me how your Mamma's doing."

Elise sat on a kitchen stool and looked around. Even as scanty as it was, it still looked clean and tidy. Fru Thoresen's kitchen was even smaller than theirs' on the third floor, but felt warm and cozy, inspite of being overcrowded. Washed clothes hung on a line over the stove, and a water bucket was on a stool in one corner with the ladle hanging in it. The scrub bucket, with a scrub brush, rag, and a wooden oval-box with green soap stood under the stool. The dustpan, the broom and an apron hung in the corner behind the door. Elise knew that

Fru Thoresen scrubbed the floors every day - down on all fours - round and round on the worn floor with soapy, hot water.

In the other corner stood a home-made stool with a tin basin and water pitcher, a chamber pot under it, and a washboard leaned against the stool. A clothes pin bag hung on the wall. There was also a rack with kettle covers hanging on a nail. The thin worn-out shawl and *skaut* of Johan's mother hung on another nail. A small, freshly ironed cotton tablecloth covered the table and the newly polished kerosene lamp stood on it.

Fru Thoresen had come from the countryside, like many of the other workers long Akerselva. Over the years, they adopted and spoke the dialect of folks on the east side of Kristiana, but had kept some words they'd brought from "home." However, both Johan and his sister, Anna, had taught themselves a "finer" language. Johan felt it would give him more possibilities to find better paid work. It was the same thing Elise's mother had said, and had instilled in both Elise and Hilda that they had to get rid of the "bad habits," as she called it.

Fru Thoresen must have noticed how she sat and thoughtfully looked around. "I try to keep it clean, at least." she sounded defensive. "You wanna *kaffesvett?*"

Elise knew she had to hurry back to her brothers, but she really wanted to talk to Johan today so she could forget about the brooch. "Thanks, just a couple drops, but I've got to go up soon."

"How's your Mamma?"

"Not good." Elise avoided looking at her. Fru Thoresen didn't look much better, thin and pale as she was, with shoulder blades protruding in her cheesecloth thin blouse, and her grey hair knotted in a tight bun. "Fru Evertsen said Mamma has been marked by death." When she heard what she'd said, a hard lump formed in her throat. Her voice was shaky and she quickly tried to blink the tears away.

"It's the best for her, Elise. She's been like this for nearly a whole year now."

Elise nodded.

"It's good that you're there for the rest of them."

Elise nodded again, still fighting back the tears. "I saw Oline get fired today." It helped to talk about something else, no matter how upsetting.

Johan's mother's nodded with a bitter look. "I could just..." She didn't say more, her lips pinched and her hands knuckled.

Elise knew what she wanted to say. Nearly everyone felt the same way about the shop foreman.

Just then they heard heavy footsteps and the door opened. Johan came rushing in.

"Elise?"

She felt herself blushing and smiled shyly. "Johan, I must talk to you about something. It's important." She looked around.

Johan's mother took the hint. "I'll look in on Anna," she said. "Say hello to your Mamma."

Elise turned to Johan as soon as his mother was gone. He stood there - tall, confident, assured, so handsome and manly it nearly hurt. "I found something today," she whispered. "Ja! Something and I don't know what to do with it."

Johan looked puzzled. "You found something?"

Elise put her hand in her apron pocket and pulled out the shiny brooch. "This," she whispered. "It was on the sidewalk.

At first I thought it was a *krone*, and nearly panicked when I realized what it was."

Johan took the brooch from her hand, stared at it a moment and looked at her. "Where did you find it?"

"Right outside here. I'm so scared someone will think I stole it. What do you think I should do with it? Should I go to the police? Or to the director? Maybe his daughter lost it."

Johan stood thinking for a moment, and then he put the brooch in his own pocket. "Elise, I'll take care of it. You don't have to think any more about it. I'll find out who owns it."

Elise stood up from the stool and threw her arms around his neck. "Thank you so much. I was so afraid I would have to go to the director I could hardly stand still at the machine today."

He put his arms around her, pulled her tightly to his chest and gave her a good hug. He smelled so good. She felt secure. Reluctantly she drew herself away from his warmth to go back up to Mamma and the others. Now she had only one problem: Hilda.

Chapter 3

When Elise came out on the landing to run up to the third floor, she stopped abruptly and listened. She thought she had heard a strange sound, but now it was quiet. When she moved towards the steps, she heard it again. It sounded like a puppy whimpering, but she had to be mistaken. Nobody in this tenement building had a puppy.

And now she heard it again! It wasn't a puppy after all, but someone crying.... She stood motionless holding her breath. Instinct told her it was Hilda, but why in the world would Hilda be hiding and crying in the stairwell instead of coming upstairs to tell her what was wrong? Carefully she tip-toed down the steps to the first level.

No one was there; the sound must have come from the basement.

"Hilda? Is it you?"

The whimpering stopped.

"I've heard you. Hilda, you can come out now!"

Something stirred in the dark. Elise heard careful steps coming up behind her. She turned and fumbled her way back upstairs. "Hilda, I know something is wrong, I just don't understand why you can't tell me," she called down to her sister.

They didn't say talk on the way up, but as soon as they were in the kitchen, Elise turned and saw Hilda's swollen, tear-stained face. "Peder. Kristian. Go into the *kammers* and check on Mamma. I need to talk to Hilda alone."

The boys obeyed reluctant, they didn't like being alone with their sick mother, so pale and lifeless in her bed.

"Out with it, Hilda!" Elise's voice was harsh. A suspicious fear had been growing stronger.

"I ain't feelin' good!" There was stubbornness in Hilda's tone of voice; she definitely wasn't ready to talk about her problems yet. Hilda sank down onto one of the kitchen stools, propped her elbows on the table, and with her head in her hands and said, "I'm freezing cold, and there's strange buzzing and ringing in my ears."

Elise sat on the other stool and looked at her. "You know what I mean," she said quietly. "There is something else. I've noticed it for a while now, so you can just as well talk about it."

Hilda avoided her eyes. "And what would that be? I should be able to keep something to myself, shouldn't I?"

"Of course. It's just that you and I have always talked about what's bothering us. Can't we talk now too about your problems? Maybe before you talked with Mamma even more than me, but now that she is sick I have to take her place. You'll have to share with me what you did with her."

"I told you, there ain't nothin' to tell!"

Elise sat quietly, gathering courage. "I'm wondering why you haven't put anything in the soaking-bucket lately."

It was as if lightening had struck the cramped little kitchen. Hilda shrank, then quickly lifted her head with a scared look and covered her mouth with her hand. Instantly she broke into hysterical crying. Her frail body trembled.

Elise let her cry, clumsily stroking her thin back. With a shudder Elise thought that Hilda was nearly as emaciated as Mamma.

After she'd stopped crying, Hilda turned her tear-streaked face towards Elise. "Please, Elise," she gasped. "Please don't tell anyone! I'll just do like Signe then..." She stopped and bit her knuckles. Elise sent her a terrified look. "You wouldn't!" she shouted.

In her mind, she pictured the frightened Signe, insane with grief, staggering along the river's edge with a long stick, searching in the foaming, churning water, on an eternal search, for that which she had thrown away. "You know you can't keep it a secret for long," she continued angrily. "It's no worse for you than anyone else. If it's what I think it is, and the guilty one won't help you, you'll be one of the many who hurry to The Crib every morning and night. It's no worse than that."

"Akk, no worse?!" Hilda snapped, "Do you know what you're talking about? Just imagine if I have to quit working at the spinning mill. What am I gonna live on? What am I gonna do with myself?"

"He should be able to help a little, whoever lured you into this situation."

Hilda stood abruptly, the stool tipped over, when she pushed away from the table. She ran to the bucket and threw up. When the worst was over, she broke into tears again. "Elise, you don't know nothin'!" Then she stormed out the door and disappeared.

Elise sat there, stunned, gazing into the air. Had someone taken Hilda with force, had she been raped...?

By the time Mamma was settled in for the night and the boys were in bed Hilda still hadn't come back. Pappa hadn't been home for several days, and Elise hoped he wouldn't come back tonight either. She was exhausted but didn't want to go to bed until Hilda was home safe again. The thoughts of Signe scared her.

Finally she heard someone on the stairs. Hilda didn't look at Elise, didn't tell her where she had been and made it clear she was keeping it all to herself. She said a quick good night and tip-toed into the *kammers* to their mother and their brothers.

Elise was so upset she couldn't sleep. She sat on a kitchen stool mulling over Hilda's "accident" and darning her brothers' socks. She wondered if she would ever know who the sinner was.

She had made up her mind to go to bed when she heard someone come up the steps again. A careful knock on the door, and Johan stuck his head in. "Can I come in, Elise?" he whispered.

She felt warmth and happiness as she stood up. "Come on in," she whispered back. "The others have gone to bed."

He came in, threw his arms around her and hugged her tightly. They stood for a long time, their arms wrapped tightly around each other. He kissed her, and she melted in his arms. He reluctantly dropped his arms, put his hand in his pocket and put something in her hand.

"Chocolate?" she whispered in disbelief. "But Johan, you shouldn't have spent your money on such," she protested weakly, her voice happy and her heart filled with delight.

His laughter was soft and gentle. "Why can't I give something special to my sweetheart? The best girl in Sagene."

She threw her arms around his neck and felt his bristly beard against her cheek.

They kissed again and he drew her towards the table, sat on a stool and pulled her onto his lap. "Now we can share - one bite for you, one bite for me."

She carefully broke the chocolate into little pieces, and put a small bit in his mouth before she took one herself. It tasted heavenly. The chocolate melted on her palate, and she smacked her lips.

She felt guilty, thinking about those asleep in the *kammers* - her sick mother and Hilda who was late with her period and feeling miserable. She thought about her brothers who had never tasted anything so good, but didn't want to spoil Johan's joy. She put another bit of chocolate on his tongue, lightly touching his lip with her finger.

He smiled a warm and comforting smile. "I know what you're thinking. Leave the last pieces for the boys. For tomorrow morning."

She snuggled into his chest. "Johan, I love you so much."

"And I'm so happy and love you, too!"

They sat quietly holding each other, glad to have some time alone, knowing they had someone to love, someone who felt the same way.

"I've been thinking about it, Elise," he said carefully. "If I could save one krone a week, that would be four kroner a month and fifty-two kroner a year. Mamma has said we could have the daybed in the kitchen until we can find a place of our own. She loves you, too, you know."

Elise was aware she was blushing. "You mean...we should get married, Johan?"

"Why not? It's what we both want, so why not!"

Elise sat quietly thinking. The thought of sharing a bed with Johan, being with him every day, seeing him across the table, hearing his voice, looking into his handsome face and his kind eyes awakened a wild desire in her. She was nearly breathless at the thought!

Then the objections started creeping in. Mamma... Peder and Kristian. Hilda.

"Hilda is old enough to take care of the boys," Johan said immediately. He must have known her thoughts.

Elise didn't say anything.

"She is sixteen, Elise."

She detected a hint of disappointment and irritation in his voice.

"I know. It's just that... You see, something has happened. Hilda's not well."

"Is she sick? She'll get over it?" He asked, concern in his voice and worry wrinkled his brow.

"I don't know. I'm scared, Johan. She reminds me of Mamma. Always freezing and feeling sick. Today I started thinking. I don't know what we'll do if she has tuberculosis, too. I don't think we can get along on only my wages."

Johan sighed. Then he hugged her tight again. "It's just the cold winter, she'll be better when the warm sun starts shining again in the spring. I ran into her this afternoon and she didn't look sick when I saw her. Don't take on problems before they happen, Elise. Maybe your father will come home if he hears you're not living here."

"He doesn't care how we're doing," Elise said, exasperated.

Johan's voice softened. "Besides, you're only moving down one floor. You can run up here every night and look after your mother and make sure the boys do their school lessons."

"But what if...?" She bit her lip and blushed. "What if I get pregnant?"

He laughed softly. "Isn't that what we want?" He put his hand inside her wool undershirt and gently caressed her breasts.

She felt tingling and desire, deep down.

He found her lips and kissed her, gently stroking first one breast, then the other. "Elise," he whispered. "I really want you!"

She felt her nipples harden and tingle. "And I want you, too," she whispered.

"Tell me you'll marry me," he whispered.

"Yes, I'll marry you, Johan. I don't want anybody else."

He drew her shirt up, gazed eagerly at her breasts before he lowered his head and let his mouth and tongue follow the same path his hand had just taken.

Elise's body moved to and from in harmony, her breasts sending signals of arousal as he flooded her with kisses and caressing. She trembled with desire.

He looked up at her and their eyes met. The flickering from the kerosene lamp gave his face a golden glow. Her feelings for him set her whole body on fire.

"This is how it will be, Elise. Every night." he added with a smile.

She smiled, having already forgotten why she had hesitated. "I can come up here before I go to work in the mornings," she mumbled, weak with longing, she leaned against him.

Suddenly a moaning came from the *kammers*. Startled, she jumped and got off his lap, tucked her shirt in and went quickly across the room and opened the *kammers* door. She tip-toed quietly to her mother's bed. Hilda and the boys were sleeping.

"What is it, Mamma?" she whispered.

"I'm so thirsty."

Elise took the cup from the dresser and put it to her mouth, supporting her back with the other hand. It went better this time; her lips didn't stick to the tin-cup.

"Thank you," she whispered and sank back into the pillows. "Is there somebody with you?"

"It's only Johan, he's going soon."

Mamma didn't reply. She seemed to be sleeping already.

When Elise came back to the kitchen, Johan had gotten up and stood in the middle of the room. "I guess I'd best be going," he said reluctantly.

Elise nodded. "Thank you for the chocolate."

He turned and put his hand on the door knob.
"Good night, Elise."
"Good night, Johan."
He went out, and she stood looking at the closed door.

Chapter 4

The next day, Hilda seemed a bit better and Elise told herself that Johan could be right. When spring came, with sunshine and warm days, Hilda was sure to be better. She'd even eaten a whole slice of bread, drank a cup of coffee and left the kitchen with no signs of nausea or dizziness.

Maybe it wasn't so bad after all.

She sighed with relief and decided to push it aside for now. There was enough to worry about without worrying about tomorrow.

Instead her thoughts returned to Johan. Her chest was bursting with joy. He wanted to marry her! Soon. Now that they'd decided to get married, he didn't want to wait! He had even said he would manage to save one krone a week. Not many were able to do that.

She pushed the coffee kettle to the side and moved the iron rings back in place on the wood stove. She poured a cup of coffee, put a piece of bread on a tin plate and went into the *kammers* to Mamma.

The boys had lit the kerosene lamp; it was still a long time until daylight. They had made their bed, and the crocheted cover on Hilda's narrow bed was neatly folded. She was so proud of them. No matter how tired they were, they always made the bed and tidied up in the mornings.

She set the food on the dresser, pulled the cheese-cloth thin curtains carefully, so they wouldn't tear more, to the side and looked out into the darkness. A star was shining brightly in the dark sky. Soon the factory sirens would start howling and calling her to another day of torture.

"Are you feeling a little better today, Mamma?"

She nodded with a thin, weak smile.

"Here's your food. Would you like me to help you?"

"No thank you, I think I'll wait a bit. Would you please empty the chamber pot for me?"

When Elise went back in the kitchen to empty the chamber pot in the utility sink, the boys were sitting at the table finishing their school lessons. "You are so helpful," she praised them. "It isn't all kids that make their bed as good as you."

Peder looked up from his book and smiled shyly. Kristian pretended as if he hadn't heard her.

Just then the factory siren howled.

"I have to run. Today it's your turn to buy milk and fish." She tied her *skaut* under her chin, and pulled her thick shawl over her shoulders. "There's a surprise for you in the newspaper on the wood box."

They both turned around quickly, Peder ran over excitedly to take a look. When he opened it, he stood gazing at what he held in his hand. "Chocolate?" he exclaimed, as if he was in paradise. "Where'd ya git it from?"

"From Johan, he wanted me to share it with you."

Kristian gave her a suspicious look. "How'd Johan git hold o' it?"

"He bought it, you silly boy."

"Evert says that Johan, he's up to somethin' all the time."

"Evert this and Evert that..." Elise said, angrily. "Last time it was Hilda running around, now it's Johan. Doesn't Evert have anything better to do than gossip? If you don't want the piece of chocolate, then I'll take it back. You don't deserve it!"

Kristian stood up quickly and grabbed it from Peder's hand. "I din't say I din't wan' it, I was just tellin' what Evert says!"

"Well, then quit listening to him from now on. I don't like to hear about snooping and gossiping." With that she hurried out and slammed the door behind her.

Rushing down the steps, she ran right into Johan, on his way back in.

"Johan?" she exclaimed in surprise. "Have you forgotten something?"

"Ja, I forgot my coffee jug."

A glimpse of light from the dim street lamp shone on his face. She could see he was smiling.

"I've started to like coffee, me, too."

She giggled and teased him, "Well, It's about time. Hurry up, I'll wait for you."

"Nah, then you'll be late. I want to look in on Anna, too, before I leave."

"Has your mother left?"

"Ja."

"Then you'll be late."

"I know, but the foreman knows my situation."

Elise looked at him, but didn't say anything. She had yet to hear of a foreman who was so understanding. "Well, I'll be going then. Say hello to Anna from me. Tell her I'll drop by tonight."

He nodded, leaned over quickly and gave her a peck on her cheek, and then she ran off.

Johan stood for a second and watched her go. He loved her so much that it hurt. If only he knew how he could help her. She deserved some help; she had a sick mother and had to look after her little brothers. She never held a grudge. The little bit of money she earned she used for her family. Her father, who should be providing for them, was staggering around at Vaterland with his drinking buddies. Where he got the money for drinking was a mystery.

He took a deep breath and turned. Elise deserved a better life. He would make sure she got it.

Elise kept her promise and went down to Johan that evening as soon as Peder and Kristian had gotten their supper, Mamma had been helped and the dishes had been washed. Hilda hadn't come home yet.

Johan and Fru Thoresen sat eating at the kitchen table. Fru Thoresen's face lit up when she saw her, "Anna's been asking for you, Elise."

"How is she?"

"Better. Thanks to Johan. My son is good as gold, he is," she added with a mother's loving glance.

Johan winked at Elise. "Have you heard the fable about *myrsnipa*?"

Elise grinned, "Ja, do you mean that drab, ugly little mother *myrsnipa* bird that met a hunter and pleaded with him not to shoot her beautiful young babies. A while later when he came out of the swamp carrying all her dead babies, she screamed that he'd promised not to shoot her babies! He said that he shot the ugliest birds he saw. The *myrsnipa* mother bird said, "Every mother thinks her babies are the best and most beautiful!" That's the way it is with most mothers, Johan. That's just the way it should be."

"Wait and see, you'll be like that, too," Fru Thoresen said with a smile.

Elise blushed and sneaked a glance at Johan. He smiled.

"Is it okay that I go in to her now?"

"You can take a little piece o' cake to her," his mother said, as she handed Elise a small plate.

Elise looked at the store-bought cake. Her mouth watered and she hurriedly looked the other way to avoid showing her temptation.

Anna was sitting in bed, pale and thin, but in the lamplight her eyes seemed big, bright and shiny. Her smile was warm.

"I've been waiting for you, Elise! Johan told me about your secret. He couldn't wait to say it! You are the best sister-in-law I could ever get and I'm so looking forward to you moving down here to us!"

Elise tried to smile. "I'm not so sure when I can. You know Mamma is so sick and the boys still need me."

"They are eight and nine years old, Elise. You mustn't spoil them so much. And even if your mother is sick you can still run upstairs and check on her whenever you want. It'll be good to have one less person there at night, as crowded as you have it now."

Elise nodded. Anna was right. It was really crowded up there, they didn't have much room. "So, how have you been, Anna?"

"Fine," Anna replied with warmth in her eyes. "I have the most caring mother and the world's best brother. He's so kind that he bought expensive medicines for me from what he gets paid at the factory. I feel much better now."

Elise stood quietly and looked at her happy face. Imagine being that happy and satisfied when she would always be bedridden. And just imagine, Johan had been able to set aside enough money for expensive medicines. No wonder Anna and their mother were proud of him.

"I just had a visit from two girlfriends," Anna continued. "When I listen to them I can't help but think God had a reason for me being paralyzed. One of them lives in Vaterland, and it's much worse than here. So many young girls are sick." She smiled nervously, "You've probably heard about it, too. Some sickness they get when they live in sin."

Elise listened intently, "What happens?"

"It starts with the legs swelling up and horrible pain. The pain and swelling go away after a while, but then red bumps appear on the arms and neck. The bumps turns into small pimples, then boils, which then turns into gaping sores. In the end they go crazy." She shook her head.Thank God Hilda had neither red bumps nor terrible pain, Elise thought and relaxed a little. "Does one of your girlfriends have this sickness?" She couldn't hold back the shock in her voice.

"No, but one of their friends does. They didn't know the name of the sickness; they call it "pain and agony." Anna lowered her voice, "They don't know a lot about it, except its terrible. If you go across Youngstorvet and continue walking along Brogaten to Lilletorvet and Kutorvet you'll see many desperate-looking women, some drink too much and are drunkards, too. They have it much worse than us, Elise. We're freezing cold and we're hungry, but we don't have painful boils covering our bodies. Besides, we have our own homes, even if it's only a kitchen and a *kammers* where we can all sleep, and we have people who love and care about us. I thank God every night that I have a mother and a big brother. Maybe even a father, but we don't know that. Mamma thinks he got left behind in some harbor, and can't get back home. I pray to God every day that a Norwegian ship will come and bring him home one day. Can you imagine how awful it would be to come back late and see your boat disappearing into the distance! Maybe he didn't have a watch, or somebody told him the wrong time. It could be that he`s in a foreign country and strange city wandering around, not knowing where to go or what to do."

Elise shook her head, thinking that Anna's father could have found another ship a long time ago if that was the explanation, but she didn't want to hurt her feelings.

Anna's face lit up. "I dreamed he came home Easter Sunday. The same day Jesus arose from the dead. I've had premonitions before, and I'm sure Pappa will come home."

"Is there something I can do for you, Anna?"

"Would you please read a little for me? Mamma is always so tired and Johan is too busy. No doubt it's because you're getting married."

"What would you like me to read?"

"I've borrowed a book by Amalie Skram."

"Amalie Skram? The one who caused such uproar with her books? Why do you want to read her books?"

"Because I think she's brave. She writes about women who are unable to love. And, she has such empathy for people."

"Elise picked up the book from the stool by the bed. The name of the book was *Sjur Gabriel*. "What's it about?" Elise asked as she sat on the edge of the bed and leafed through the book.

"It's about poverty, illness and the human destruction caused by alcohol. She wrote about life in Bergen, but it could have just as easily been about Vaterland or Sagene. It's just as bad all over."

Elise started reading and Anna lay back on her pillows, listening attentively. Elise got so caught up in the story and read several pages without looking up. Then she noticed that Anna had fallen asleep. She didn't have the strength to stay awake, no matter how much she wanted to.

Elise put the book on the stool next to the uneaten cake, and tiptoed quietly out of the *kammers*.

Johan and his mother were still sitting by the wobbly kitchen table, with the freshly ironed little tablecloth. Johan had taken his black clay pipe out of his pocket, filled it and lit up. Thick, heavy smoke filled the small kitchen. It smelled so good.

"How was it with her, then?" Fru Thoresen looked at her eagerly.

"She's asleep. I read to her from *Sjur Gabriel* and she fell asleep."

Johan laughed. "Maybe you should have read from *En Glad Gutt*?"

"Come and sit down, Elise. Have a *kaffeskvett* with us." Fru Thoresen set out a cup, missing a handle, poured some coffee and shuffled back to the cook stove with the coffee pot.

Elise glanced at Johan through the tobacco smoke. He was wearing the same *busserullen* he always wore. She followed his hands as he lit his pipe again. Something about his hands and movements sent a quivering sensation through her body.

He glanced up from his pipe and looked at her. When their eyes met, she felt an electrifying excitement rush through her body. He smiled at her, she smiled at him!

Fru Thoresen sat down again and looked from one to the other. "Have you talked to the minister yet?"

John laughed. "Mamma, what's the hurry?! I've just told you that Elise and I are engaged and already you're talking about the minister."

Elise saw how his mother dropped her shoulders and looked ashamed over her impatience. Maybe she was looking forward to getting some help, Elise thought. A strong, young woman in the house. His mother wasn't young anymore and it wasn't easy to stand twelve to fourteen hours a day in the factory, then buy food on the way home, cook meals, wash clothes, scrub the floors and take care of a paralyzed daughter. "I have to talk to Mamma first," Elise added quickly. "Maybe she wants me to wait for a little while, until Peder and Kristian can manage without me."

Fru Thoresen snorted, "Peder and Kristian? Aren't they eight and nine years old? Well, let me tell ya! When I was nine years old, I was already workin' after school in the match factory, thirty-six hours a week. It was lots o' dust and really noisy, much worse than today. Many workers got very sick. It was the phosphor they made matches with - many got so sick that they threw up, got yellow skin and some got burns inside o' their mouths and their jaws rotted away. That's how it was then. They got it much better today."

"Today it's against the law to let kids work in the factories before they're twelve years old," Johan added. "And kids between twelve and fourteen can't work more than six hours a day."

"Well, we did and it din't hurt non'of us." His mother pinched her lips together in irritation. "Ya gotta learn to work hard if you're gonna make it in this life. "Idleness is the root of all evil," like the minister says. Hangin' out on street corners and getting' into trouble is what happens when they got too much time to do nothin'."

"They don't have time for school and school lessons when they work all day at the factory," Johan objected. "You'll get nowhere in life without an education. The factory owners use children and young people as cheap labor. Their excuse is that to be able to compete, they have to because it's done that way in other countries."

Elise glanced over at Johan.

"And they're ruining their health," he continued. "It's not good for our society."

"You're talkin' just like the minister and them folks in the Salvation Army," his mother mumbled. "A little more coffee, Elise?"

"No, thank you. I've got to get upstairs. Hilda wasn't home yet when I came down here."

"O', ja, what's goin' on with her then?" His mother looked at her with concern.

"What's going on with her? Nothing that I know of." Elise felt her face getting red. "Well, I mean, she's always cold and not feeling so good, but it's the same for most of us this time of the year."

"She ain't got TB - her, too?!"

"I hope it's not that." Elise got up. "Thanks for the coffee."

"You can follow her up, then, Johan."

Johan quickly stumped out his pipe and got up from the kitchen stool. His mother lit a kerosene lamp and handed it to him.

He sat the lamp down on the floor the minute they were outside and threw his arms around her. "Elise, I love you so much," he whispered into her ear. "See if you can convince your mother. I can't wait a whole year, let alone two."

"I don't think I can, either," she whispered before she felt his lips against hers.

"This is absolutely the greatest thing a person could experience," she thought. Not even the director's grand house in Oscarsgate, his daughter's beautiful clothes, or his new "automobile" could measure up to loving someone and knowing you were loved in return. She was filled with happiness; it made her feel lighter, as if floating on air.

And now she wished she could be held in Johan's arms for the rest of her life, feel his lips on hers, his strong, safe arms around her and feel with her whole being that he was filled with the same longing for her. What did it matter that they didn't have money for their own place when they could sleep on the daybed in his mother's kitchen? The most important thing was they had each other, that they would sleep in the same bed, eat at the same table, run hand in hand down the steps on their way to work in the factories and look forward to being together after the factories closed for the night.

She was luckier than most. There weren't many girls who had found the one they wanted to share their lives with. Too many had babies without knowing who the father was. The Crib on the other side of Beierbrua was living proof of that.

He eased his grip. "I could stand like this all night," he whispered in her ear. "But then, I'm sure your mother wouldn't let you marry me."

She laughed softly. "Maybe not. Oh, how I wish I could be here with you all night, too," she added with a small sigh. "If only Hilda would get well again, then she could take care of Peder and Kristian."

"She'll get better, Elise. And Mamma's right; the boys are big enough to take care of themselves. At least as long as you are only one floor below them."

She laughed softly again; her chest swelling with happiness. "I think I've always known I was going to share my life with you, Johan. I didn't ever think the other boys were interesting. I used to adore you like a brother, but now…"

"But now?" His voice was both teasing and anxious.

"I never noticed anything until spring last year. All of a sudden I was nervous when you talked to me. It was so strange."

"Are you nervous now, too?" He let his hand slide over her breasts.

She didn't answer, just closed her eyes and felt the sweet sensation run through her body.

"You're not telling me what you're feeling right *now*," he whispered in a deep voice.

"Do you think I need to?" she whispered back.

They heard a door open into the back yard and jumped away from each other.

"Come," he said as he took her hand and started up the steps.

"I hope it's Hilda."

"I thought you hoped no one would come."

"I did hope that, too."

"Hilda's probably been standing in some dark stairway necking with Lorang, the errand boy."

Elise didn't respond. Suddenly, she remembered Hilda's expression when she had mentioned the soaking bucket. She forced that thought to the side.

She still hadn't asked Johan what he had done with the brooch. But s he didn't want to ruin this special moment. Maybe he had lost his courage and hadn't turned it in yet? He might be embarrassed and humiliated if she asked him.

Johan knew the director. He had worked in the spinning mill before he started working at Seilduk, the canvas factory. The director had been more considerate towards Johan than to everyone else, probably because he'd appreciated Johan's maturity. Johan would certainly go to him instead of the police. She didn't think the director would be suspicious and think Johan had stolen it.

If he had turned it in, he would have said so.

They heard light steps below.

"I think it's Hilda," she said, relieved. She hadn't thought Hilda would do anything foolish, but you never know. You heard all kinds of strange things. Signe had dropped her baby in the river, and then blamed it on slipping on the ice saying it fell out of her arms, but those who knew her didn't believe her. She had threatened to get rid of it, had said the baby would be an anchor around her feet. So, she'd found the solution in the rapid, frothy river.

Others had gone to a secret place in Møllergate, and come back with empty stomachs... She shuddered at the thought. Some had died a few days later, the blood in their beds told their painful stories.

"We have many evenings ahead of us, Elise," Johan whispered softly. "This stairwell is ours, and it isn't often that anyone goes here so late at night."

They had reached the third floor.

"Thanks for coming up with me, Johan. I'll see you tomorrow morning."

"I have to leave early, but I'll see you tomorrow night."

Hilda had caught up to them.

"There you are, Hilda. I was beginning to worry about you."

Hilda didn't say a word, just sneaked past them, opened the kitchen door and disappeared inside without closing it behind her. A soft light shone from the kitchen.

"What is with her?" Johan asked.

Elise looked down. "I said she's not feeling well."

"And still she's out running around long into the night?"

Elise didn't answer.

"Good night, Elise."

"Good night, Johan."

She stood in the doorway for a minute so the kerosene lamp in the kitchen would light Johan's way. He took the steps two at a time, soon she heard that his door close.

When Elise came in, Hilda stood still and looked at her with a strange expression.

"I've decided to tell you," remoteness in her voice, yet more determined and somewhat harder than usual.

"It's the *verksmester*..."

Chapter 5

Elise wrinkled her brow, confused. "What are you saying?! What do you mean?!"

"Don't pretend. You know exactly what I mean!"

But Elise did not know! Had Johan told Hilda about the brooch? Had the director told the *verksmester* and it really was the director's daughter who'd lost it? Or, did it belong to someone else?

"Don't stand there and pretend you don't understand!" Hilda's voice was agitated and loud. "Have you forgotten what you said to me? You said if a guy knocks-up a girl, he should help. You did say that!"

Elise's scalp tingled and the hairs on her head stood straight up on end, a chill wave swept across her face. She opened her mouth to say something, but couldn't find words-- nothing came out. She stared at her sister, thoughts racing through her head.

"Don't you understand anything?!" Hilda's voice was rising. Lightning flashed in her eyes. "You're so perfect; always do what Mamma tells you. You don't get into hopeless trouble, you have Johan. You know what you want and have your life in order, even if you've been at the spinning mill longer than me and know what happens to us. Even if you know Signe was like a lunatic wandering along the river, with a long stick, trying to find her baby she'd thrown in. Even if you know that the life along the Akerselva is terrible and unbearable. Especially when your father is a drunk, your mother has TB and this rat's nest of a place we live in stinks like piss all the time and there's critters crawling out of the walls. You know just as well as I do, the rich get richer and the poor get poorer. That's how it is in this world.

Yep, now it's my turn. But, I'm in good company, who knows how many other girls from Hjula and Vøien have done the same thing before me!"

Elise looked hard at her, not understanding. She didn't get half of what Hilda was saying, but she had an idea what she meant by the last part. When she finally managed to say something, she dumbfoundly asked, "Are you sure? I mean, you've been late before, and..."

Hilda laughed a harsh and bitter laughter that Elise hadn't heard before. "Open your eyes, Elise!"

Elise tried to think if she'd noticed anything different about Hilda, with the exception that she looked pale and depressed, but she could not think clearly. Usually Hilda crept under the covers before her, and she dressed in the morning in the other corner of the kitchen while Elise built the fire in the woodstove and made coffee. "What about the fever? Couldn't it be something else that's wrong with you?"

"Would it be better if I had TB? Or that I ended up in the fourth ward at Ullevaal Hospital, locked up for weeks, months and years, with sores covering my whole body?" Hilda's eyes were black with bitterness and hate. Hate towards the factory owners, hate towards men with authority, and hate towards the rich, Elise thought. Lives of the factory workers living on the wrong side of the river were devastated, not only by poverty, but by the rich misusing their power.

"Don't talk that way," Elise was on the verge of tears. "I'll help you, Hilda. We'll get along somehow. Kristian can start to work, too. He could be an errand boy, like Lorang, since he's not old enough to work at the factory."

She could have bit off her tongue when she mentioned Lorang's name. Hilda's face turned hard and bright red, she turned sharply on her heals and disappeared into the *kammers*. Elise caught a glimpse of her as she threw herself onto her mattress, her frail and thin body shook, crying without sound. Thank goodness, Mamma was asleep.

Elise closed the door slowly, sat down at the kitchen table and stared into thin air. How could she marry Johan when Mamma has tuberculosis, Hilda was having a baby and Kristian more than likely would have to start working? They're old enough to take care of themselves Johan's mother had said, but she didn't know Peder and Kristian like she did. Peder, meek and sensitive, who cried easily and needed a grownup for support, Kristian, the extreme opposite, hard and distant, easily lured to running with the boys in the streets. Mamma had done all she could to keep her boys away from it.

If he didn't have someone there to support him, too, he could start hanging out at beer-joints, start stealing to get money for "moon-shine" and even get arrested. She knew too many who had ended up like that. No, she couldn't leave her brothers to themselves.

Johan's mother had grown up in a different time, when kids under twelve worked at the factory from morning until night with "no time for mischief" as she had said. Elise did not want *that* time to come back. She was happy that Peder and Kristian didn't have to do that now. Fru Thoresen didn't understand why boys aged eight and nine needed looking after. She'd never needed to worry about it, either.

If only Pappa had been the father he should be… She sighed heavily. She stood up wearily from the kitchen stool, lit the lantern to go down to the outhouse before going to bed.

It was quiet in the stairwell, all were most likely sleeping. When she came down to the second floor, she noticed clumps of snow on the steps. Maybe Johan or his mother had been down before her.

The thought of Johan made her both happy and sad. He would be disappointed, yes frustrated, and maybe angry, when he heard that she couldn't marry him yet. Should she dare tell him about Hilda? All she had to say was that Hilda was pregnant; she didn't have to tell him who the father is. He would think its Lorang, the errand boy, but it was okay if he thought that. To tell the truth could be risky.

Johan was confident, sure of himself. Maybe he was a bit too confident at times. He would be furious if he heard the truth. Hilda was only sixteen, after all. Maybe he would storm into the *verksmester's* office, pound on his desk and tell him a thing or two! But that would lead to nothing but more trouble. Maybe she and Hilda would even get fired. And what would happen to them then - with no jobs?

New falling snow hit her face when she opened the door to the backyard. The footprints were already covered with new snow. She had to run past the trash cans to get to the outhouse, she heard rooting-around sounds from them. So the rats were back. She usually kicked the can, flipped the cover off and moved quickly to the side before she threw the garbage in so the rats could come out first. She hated the greedy, ugly beasts with their long, disgusting tails. Once an ugly, fat rat had come running straight at her. She'd thrown everything she had in her hands and ran. She hadn't had the guts to look back, but ran as fast as she could, imagining the rat would sink his sharp teeth into her heels at any moment. Shivers ran down her back thinking about it.

It was bitterly cold. She should have put her boots on before running down, now her toes were frostbitten again. Her feet were wet, too. As soon as she was done, she put the hook on the door and ran back, cold shooting through her.

56

She had nearly reached the second landing when she heard someone at the outside gate. So strange that someone was out at this time of night, she thought. Quick footsteps came behind her, she slowed down. The footsteps sounded like Johan's. She stopped and turned around.

"Johan?"

He came up quickly behind her in the dark, she knew it was him. A moment later she was in his arms.

"I had to run an errand for Mamma. When I heard somebody in the steps, I wanted it to be you. You're so cold, Elise. You're freezing." He hugged her tightly to his chest and rubbed her back. "After we're married, I'll keep you warm every night. You'll lay so close to me that you'll never, ever shiver again from the cold."

She smiled and snuggled against his chest. "It'll be wonderful, Johan."

After she went to bed it wasn't thoughts about nights with Johan, but overwhelming thoughts about Hilda's problems. She couldn't fall asleep. She felt overwhelmed with problems piling up, like a thick, impregnable wall. Hilda was pregnant. With the *verksmester*! It was impossible to imagine. She had done it voluntarily, on top of it all, or had she really? Could it be that he had raped her and for whatever reason she refused to talk about it? Or had she seduced him, in hopes that he would help them out of poverty? And later understood he absolutely would have nothing to do with her and the baby? Or maybe he didn't even know about it?

What will Johan say when she tells him she can't marry him after all? At least not until after Hilda's baby was born, and she saw how they were doing. If Hilda was lucky she would be able to keep her job and like all the other unwed mothers bring the baby to The Crib every day. Everything depended on her health. She said a silent prayer that Hilda's fever and dizziness were only a regular winter cold and had nothing to do with tuberculosis.

But, what would they do if Hilda lost her job? It had happened to several others. She heard The Frog's voice resonating in her ears. "Absolutely not! If you play, you pay!" Besides it was a long way up to The Crib. How would Hilda ever come all the way up there before she had to be at the mill?

When Elise woke up the next morning she discovered to her disbelief that Hilda's bed was empty. She got up quickly and tip-toed out of the *kammers*. Peder and Kristian weren't awake yet and from Mamma's bed in the corner, no sound could be heard.

No one was in the kitchen. The fire hadn't been started in the woodstove, the kerosene lamp wasn't warm. Hilda must have dressed in the dark and snuck out. What was she doing out in the snowy weather? It was only five o'clock in the morning, still an hour before the factory sirens began to howl.

She took the water bucket and poured water in the wash basin. The water was freezing cold on her face; she shivered, dried herself quickly and pulled her shirt over her head. Today she had to build a fire in the stove in the *kammers*. They'd agreed to save on coal as long as possible, but the temperatures had been below freezing three days now. It wasn't healthy for Mamma to lie in the cold room all day.

When she opened the wood box, she discovered there was no firewood left. Irritated she opened the door to the *kammers*, and called to Kristian. He came immediately, sleepy and grumpy, but he probably heard the tone in her voice and knew it was best to come right away. When you forgot to bring in wood, you didn't get breakfast!

With fingers stiff from the cold, she set out bread, butter and syrup. At the same time, Peder came pattering into the kitchen and started getting dressed. "Why's it so cold in 'ere?" he shivered.

"Because Kristian forgot to carry in wood."

"Where's Hilda?"

"I don't know."

"You don' know?" He stopped, looking at her with fear in his eyes.

She shook her head. "She got up before me." When she saw the anxiousness in his face, she hurriedly forced a smile, "Maybe she was meeting somebody."

"Lorang, you mean?"

Elise shrugged her shoulders. "Apparently you know more about that than I do."

He nodded and grinned. "Dey is sweethearts. I saw 'em down in da street." He blushed and looked quickly towards the floor. "Dey was kissin'."

"You'll be doing that, too, when you are sixteen."

"Yuk, no! Kissin,' no way! Darned if I will."

"It's not nice to swear, Peder."

"I wadn't swearin.' Sayin' Jesus and Oh m'God and hell—dat's swearin!' Dat's whad 'em folk at da Salvation Army says."

Elise didn't say anything. She wasn't quite sure what "darned" meant, and thought maybe he was right. "Get dressed and run down to help Kristian. Maybe no wood had been chopped."

Kristian came in a moment later with an armful of wood. A loud crashing sound filled the room when he dumped it into the wood box.

Elise quickly crumpled a page from an old newspaper, put it and a couple pieces of kindling in the woodstove, lit it, and set the coffee kettle over it. "Today you can make your school lunches yourselves. I'm going in to help Mamma."

Immediately when she went into the *kammers*, she had an uncomfortable feeling that something was different. She lit the kerosene lamp on the dresser and glanced over at Mamma's brown-painted bed. She lay motionless, her eyes were closed, but her breathing wasn't as heavy as usual. Elise didn't hear any breathing at all.

Elise was gripped with fear. "Mamma?"

Then she saw Mamma's lips move ever so slightly and she breathed a shallow breath. Quietly she went over to her. "Are you awake, Mamma?"

Mamma moved her head slowly to the side, but didn't open her eyes. She coughed a dry, sharp wheezing sound that cut through Elise's heart like a knife. After the coughing stopped, she started to breathe heavily again, just as she'd done these last few days. Without a warning, she raised a thin, pale hand and fumbled towards Elise, it lay cold and gnarled on her sleeve. "It's so sad and lonely laying here all alone, Elise," Her voice strained. "The day gets so long."

"It's soon morning, Mamma. In about an hour it'll start to get light. And I'll come home during lunch break, like I usually do. Would you like a little coffee?"

Mamma weakly shook her head. "Just a little water." Her voice was faint.

Elise hurried into the kitchen to get water from the bucket. The boys sat by the table, making breakfast and their school lunches. It warmed her heart to see they were so well-behaved. "You didn't see Hilda when I was in with Mamma, did you?"

They shook their heads without looking up.

"Will you have a little bread?" she asked when she came back to Mamma's bed.

Mamma shook her head.

"You haven't eaten much for many days."

"I'm not up to it, Elise." Now her voice was merely a whisper.

Elise sat on the edge of her bed, held the cup to her lips, but Mamma turned her head away.

"You said you would have a little water." Her mother shook her head.

Elise put the cup on the dresser. "I'm to bring you greetings from Fru Thoresen," she started cautiously. "I was down and said hello to Anna last night."

Mamma didn't say anything, but Elise had a feeling she was listening.

"Anna is a lovely girl. She called herself lucky because she has a kind mother and a wonderful big brother and said that many have it much worse than she does."

Mamma blinked her eyes.

"She said Johan is the kindest person in the whole world. He even used some of his wages to buy expensive medicines for her."

Mamma nodded weakly.

Elise hesitated a second, then decided she wanted to tell Mamma now! "Johan has asked me to marry him!" She held her breath waiting for Mamma's reaction.

Her spirits lightened, she saw a tiny smile glide over Mamma's pale and colorless lips. "You remember what I said?" Mamma exerted.

"Ja, and I said I couldn't marry my big brother," Elise smiled. "I saw him like a brother. Until last summer."

Another weak smile slid over Mamma's dry lips; apparently she had known it all along.

"I can't get a better man than Johan." She wanted to say more. "You know what, Mamma? He's even managing to save one *krone* every week. That's fifty-two *kroner* a year. I don't know how he can do it, but he does."

She stopped for a minute, hoping Mamma would say something, like suggesting they didn't have to wait, but she didn't.

"Fru Thoresen has offered us the daybed in the kitchen until we find our own little place. Just up one set of steps and I can be here in a wink. I can come up every morning and night, help you and make sure Peder and Kristian do their school lessons."

To her surprise Mamma began to move her head from side to side and a deep wrinkled frown filled her forehead.

"I won't do it if you don't want me to, Mamma," she quickly added to calm her. "It's really okay – I can wait until you're well again."

She saw wetness sneaking out from under Mamma's eyelashes and tears slid slowly down over her thin, hollow cheeks.

"Mamma, please don't cry!" Elise was distressed. "I won't do it! I can wait until Kristian gets a job."

Her mother moved her head slowly, at the same time a small hiccup sound came from her dried, cracked lips. In the next second, her lips moved. She thought Mamma whispered, "Say yes to Johan, Elise," but she wasn't sure.

The factory siren howled and she stood up, "Try to get some sleep. I'll be back soon."

"Kristian, Peder..." she said, as soon as she was back in the kitchen, "can you look in on Mamma before you go to school? Ask her if she'll have some bread or a cup of coffee. The coffee kettle is still warm."

Peder looked at her with huge, frightened eyes. "Is Mamma gonna die, Elise?"

"Uff, who said something like that?"

"Evert!" Kristian said, in a loud and clear voice.

Elise felt the anger rising. "I will not hear one word more about Evert! Evert is just upset because he can't go to school, and he's taking it out on you."

Both of them lowered their heads in shame and didn't say another word.

Elise had hoped to run into Johan in the stairwell, but didn't see anything of him. He had said he needed to leave early, but she could still hope.

Three young workers walked ahead of her, dressed in worn out leather pants, *busseruller* and *skyggelua* on their heads. They had coffee bottles in their pockets and walked with a mannish gait. They spit brown licorice and talked loud, especially when they swore. Elise only caught a few words: "Damn," "get outa the way," and "go to hell." It was strange she thought that boys always had to swear to prove they were men.

Then she snapped up some words that made her eyes widen, and she listened. She had heard the name: "Turd-Anders." Turd-Anders had sailed in the merchant marines with Johan when they were fifteen years old, and they both had signed-off after a year at sea. While Johan went to work immediately at the factory, Turd-Anders was lazy and thought the world owed him a living. He started drinking, and totally messed up his life.

Now he was one of the worst street bums. He had been in the "Criminal" in Trondheim several times, in Akershus Federal Prison for prisoners serving long term sentences, and had lived in Ingebrigtens Hotel in Vognmandsgate where many street-girls lived. A rumor had gone around that he'd put some of the "girl's" takings in his own pockets, but she wasn't sure it was true. He'd gotten his nick-name after he said it was better hanging out with the "turds" than "the uppity-ups." What had Turd-Anders been up to now? She wondered and hastened her gait to hear better.

Her feet crunched on the hard frozen sidewalk. She was freezing cold and pulled her shawl tighter around her body. When she cut kitty-corner across the street, she had to hold herself from tripping in the frozen ruts of the sled tracks.

She hadn't been able to see if she knew any of the young workers, but now they were turning down towards the bridge. Just then she heard them laughing loudly, and caught a few incoherent words: "the delivery bike" and "keep a look out." At the same time some girls going to the spinning mill came from another direction, and the boys' conversation faded, and they walked on.

The roar from the waterfalls grew louder, and it was impossible to hear what anyone on the bridge was saying. The only sound that could be heard over the rushing river and the gushing waterfalls was the noise from the blacksmith shop, where the blacksmith's anvil machines were already pounding. The sound cut sharply in her ears, even though she'd tucked her shawl tightly around her head.

She had just crossed over the bridge and swung down towards the factory gate when she heard someone shouting behind her: "Elise?"

She turned towards the voice. It was Valborg. Nosey Valborg!

"Whad was Johan doin'leavin' so early this mornin'?"

"How would I know?"

"Well, you are engaged!"

"Who said that?"

"Johan."

Elise didn't believe her ears. She couldn't imagine that Johan had gone around telling others before she'd said yes, and it was only two days ago. Last night she had been with him and the night before he had been with her. There was no way he could have had time to tell anyone but his mother and sister. It was too noisy during work hours and so much work that the workers didn't have time to chat.

"You need to keep a closer eye on 'im, Elise. If I'd been so lucky to catch a guy like 'im, I wodn't slip 'im outa my sight for a secon'."

"Stop your nonsense!" Elise felt her heart pounding in anger. "If there is one person in the world I trust, it is Johan!"

Valborg laughed. "Dat's whad ya t'ink! But I know somethin' you don' know... The girls hang after 'im like flies, and don' come and tell me he don' like it!"

To Elise's exasperation, she couldn't resist turning to get back at her. "You're a big liar! They can hang around him all they want. He could care less about them."

Valborg laughed again. "Do really ya t'ink I'm dat dum' dat I believe ya?"

Elise turned her back to her, lifted her chin and walked with swift steps to the gate.

At that moment the night watchman was on his way out. "Gosh, so fuming mad you look today, Elise," he exclaimed and smiled at her.

Refusing to look at him, she raged past and up the steps to the spinning mill. He'd flirted all autumn and refused to give up, no matter how much she openly avoided and ignored him.

She was one of the first to come into the hall; the machines had not been turned on yet. But the other working girls started streaming in and soon the work would begin.

Elise searched for Hilda, but couldn't find her. She must not be late for work. If she arrived only a few minutes past six o'clock, she'd be locked out and docked in pay. The doors didn't open again until nine o'clock and she would have to stand outside in the cold for three hours. Elise didn't think she'd risk going home to Mamma. It had happened once before, when Mamma was still well, and she'd been anything but sympathetic.

She still didn't see Hilda and her thoughts wandered to Valborg and all the dumb things she had said. She'd said them to harass her. Valborg was jealous and envious, which was easy to understand, but did she have to be so nasty about it? Elise knew Valborg had a crush on Johan for a long time. She had told this one and that one. But how did she find out that Johan and she were planning to get married?

Maybe she knew some of Anna's girlfriends? Anna had been so happy, and even if she didn't intend to gossip, maybe she'd let it slip out. That had to be the reason. There wasn't much excitement at Sagene, so when one of the workers was getting married the news spread like wildfire. There wasn't much else to talk about other than the usual complaints of being tired and worn out, sickness and worries about paying the rent and the sky-high rocketing prices of food.

She decided to forget about Valborg and concentrate on her work. She was distinctly aware that she hadn't slept well during the night and as time crawled at a snail's pace, it became harder and harder to concentrate on the threads. She felt herself on the verge of nodding off a couple of times and forced herself to keep her eyes open. Her back ached, and warmth hadn't returned to her toes. After being frost bitten they had started to ache, so much that she could hardly stand still. Her hands were red and cracked from the cold weather and the cold water. Scrubbing the steps, scrubbing potatoes, scrubbing clothes and scrubbing the floors, and taking the stiff-frozen clothes down from the clothesline didn't make it any better. She tried to comfort herself with thoughts about being on the right side of Christmas, warmer days were on the way and since she'd gotten through all the other cold winters, she could hold out this year too.

Hilda arrived at nine o'clock. She didn't look in Elise's direction, just rushed to her place without looking left or right, and flew between the machines as soon as they started up again. Elise was so relieved to see her, yet at the same time wondered where she had been and worried that she wouldn't be observant enough. It was dangerous to have other thoughts in your head when you were a bobbin girl. If her frock got caught in the machine, she would be done for. They had heard horrible stories about bobbin girls who'd gotten too close to the wheels.

Swirling dust filled the work hall, and hung like smoke clouds up under the ceiling. The sweeping women didn't clean until the machines stopped at the end of the day; there was no point in it because in a couple minutes it would be just as unbearable again. Several of the girls suffered with eye infections and had to lay home covering their eyes with cloths soaked in boric acid solution, and suffering with thoughts of their dwindling pay.

Finally it was lunch time. Only those who lived close by went home during the break, all the others ate at the factory. As soon as the machines stopped, lunch buckets were heard clanging in the hallway. All who stayed got a cup of soup, which they ate with their own tin spoons, brought from home. Elise was happy she didn't have to take a cut in pay for the soup, besides she had to go home and look after Mamma. She looked down to the other end of the hall, and got Hilda's attention; she waved for Elise to go. Apparently she was eating soup at the mill today. Elise was filled with curiosity when she left. Where had Hilda been, and why wouldn't she go home with her?

The cold struck sharply when she came out. Shivering, she pulled her coarsely, handknit shawl tighter around her. She stopped in the middle of the bridge and stared down at the foul smelling river. Wisps of misty frost drifted over the surface of the water. The river stopped up here and formed a small undisturbed pond before gushing over the falls. Fog floated along the river banks, a thin layer of ice already forming on the surface.

She looked towards the powerful, rumbling waterfalls. Over the years more than one person had been lured by the greenish-brown swirling waters and jumped... She recoiled with a shudder and pulled her eyes away.

Footsteps came behind her, as she crossed over to the other side. The snow forced its way through the holes in her boots, and ice cold snow came swirling down from the rooftops. Ah, to be in a warmer country...

Her throat tightened when she hurried up the steps at home. The same terrible fear that something was wrong, which she'd felt this morning, came over her again. Apprehensively she opened the door to the kitchen.

Chill hadn't filled the room yet, there was a little warmth from firing up this morning. The boys had cleaned off the table and wiped away the breadcrumbs. She went to the wood box, about to stoke the fire first, but stopped. What did it help to delay facing the problem, sooner or later she had to. She carefully opened the door to the *kammers*.

"Mamma...?"

There was no answer. Her heart beat hard and fast between her ribs. "Mamma...?" she repeated a little louder, but again there was no answer. She took a deep breath, pulled her shoulders back, straightening her back, and stepped in.

So, it had happened, she thought. The skin on Mamma's face was transparent, her eyes closed and on her thin, bony hands blue blood vessels threaded the surface. Now she had finally found peace...

Then there was some movement under the covers. Mamma's hands shifted a little, one clutching a wrinkled handkerchief. Mamma had always been so particular about having clean, freshly ironed handkerchiefs. Elise moved quietly towards the bed.

"Mamma? Are you sleeping?"

Her mother moved her head weakly without answering.

"Did Peder and Kristian give you breakfast?"

Mamma nodded and blinked her eyes. Just then Elise noticed the tinplate on the dresser. A small half-eaten piece of bread laid there, she couldn't have taken many bites. Elise picked up the coffee cup. It was cold, but sweet and better than just water. "Take a small swallow, Mamma, so your mouth won't be so dry," she encouraged her and held the cup to her lips. To her relief Mamma drank the little that was left.

"I'm stoking up the fire," she continued in the same encouraging voice. "It's been below freezing three days now, and we have enough coal." The last part was only partially true, but Mamma didn't need more worries.

She got some kindling and a couple small chunks of wood and soon the fire burned lively in the stove. She lifted the coal pail and dumped in some coal. It should be nice and warm for Mamma today. She stood momentarily and looked blankly down at the worn wooden floor planks, her thoughts spinning. Hilda hadn't seemed the least bit upset when she waved her to leave. Rather the opposite. It was so strange that she had gotten up earlier than she needed to this morning, then disappeared without saying anything, been late for work and still looked happy in the lunch break. She shook her head, confused, and when she was sure the fire wouldn't go out she hurried into the kitchen to build a fire in the cookstove, too. She took the oatmeal from the cupboard, poured water in the kettle and cooked oatmeal-*grøt*, so she'd saved money for dinner today, too.

It was agonizing leaving the apartment after the lunch break. Her mother was going downhill. One day it wouldn't be only fright that stopped her...

She stopped for a moment on the bridge again. She just couldn't stop herself. She stood by the rusty iron railing and looked down towards the waterfall. Icicles had formed on the sides, and the frost mist lay even thicker than a little while ago. She thought about the man who'd slipped on the ice and slid under the railing straight down into the river. It was said it had been an accident, but she wasn't so sure.

Folks hurried past her, women with shawls crossed over their chests and tied at their backs, huddled over, their heads lowered into the wind. They were going in the direction of the huge brick buildings, which stood there, dark and imposing, stretching their brick chimneys towards a frosty cold sky. Without the river, they would not be standing there.

The factory existed only because of this river named Akerselva, it ran the turbines, the axles and the pulleys, and everything else factories needed. The water powered everything. Because of the water, the factory existed. As well as all the sore, cracked and weary women's hands. Without them there would be no spinning mills or weaving mills. Without them the director wouldn't be living in his elegant apartment with many rooms in Oscarsgate nor driving his automobile.

She pulled away from the iron railing and hurried after the others down towards the factory. A new work shift was waiting for her.

Chapter 6

Finally the factory siren howled. Then came the sirens from the other factories, each with a slightly different sound, and then another, it sounded like the siren at Seilduken. That meant Johan was done for the day, too.

The girls streamed out of the hall, pale and weak from exhaustion. Elise saw her own misery, tiredness, hunger, cold and lack of sleep mirrored in their faces. She thought about Anna, lying in her bed, day in and day out, in the small dark *kammers*, quiet and helpless, and yet always talking about how lucky she was. She, who would never experience the joy of being kissed by a boy she loved, never be married, never have children, never lie in the warm moss, staring up into the cloudless summer sky, listening to the birds chirping and smelling the fragrance of flowers. Everyone walking here, no matter how tired and hungry, was lucky in comparison to Anna. "It's not what you have, but what you do with what you have," her mother used to say before she got sick. Anna was a living example of that.

I should be comparing myself with Anna rather than with the director's daughter, she thought. Comparing your life with someone who has it worse, you'll be grateful instead of bitter. She had heard enough stories about the street-girls down in Vaterland, about the girls on the fourth ward at Ullevaal Hospital with venereal disease, and about the drunken street-girls locked up Mangelsgården, and not even able to go to their mothers' or fathers' funerals without the shame of having a constable by their side. No, when she compared herself to them she was one of the lucky ones.

Anyway, she didn't have to make such comparisons, she had Johan!

It'd been a long time since she had heard the waterfalls rushing as loudly as today. The cold bit her nose; it went straight through her winter shawl and the rough material in her clothes. It stung her skin, penetrated through to her bones, sent shivers of cold up her spine, ached in her ribs, arms and legs, like a nagging toothache. She hated the winter. When she and Johan became rich, they would embark on one of the huge steamships she had seen in the harbor and sail away to warmer lands. And they would live there for the rest of their lives.

The thought made her smile. She imagined herself like a lady she'd seen on a postcard, wearing a billowy, flowing white dress and a straw hat, swaying palm trees in the background.

Darkness had set in. The gas lamps were lit on Sandakerveien. Snowflakes danced in the lights like small elves dressed all in white. Thank God, Peder and Kristian were home so Mamma wasn't alone. Maybe Hilda was home, too. She had not seen her when everybody piled out of the factory, but it wasn't easy to recognize anyone in the stream of hundreds of dark-clad women. At least not when the winter darkness had settled over the city and the misty frost hung over the bridge.

She wondered if Johan had come...

Just then she heard quick steps coming up behind her. She turned her head.

In the low light from the gas lamp she spotted Hilda. Her face was red and she seemed happily excited, even though she must be feeling miserable.

"Where in the world were you this morning?" Elise heard both curiosity and scolding in her voice.

"I've got something to tell you, Elise." Her voice sounded unusually happy and carefree.

Elise stopped inspite of being very cold. Yesterday, Hilda had been so sick that she thought she had tuberculosis, like Mamma, and she had thrown herself on the bed, crying, after she had admitted to her 'condition.' "Is everything okay again then?" she asked with skepticism.

"No, I'm still coughing and have a fever, but it'll go away. There is something else, Elise. Something you just won't believe!"

Elise was so cold her teeth were chattering. "I'm so cold, can't this wait until we are home and inside?"

Hilda didn't say anything and they walked faster.

It wasn't until they were in the narrow stairwell between the first and second floor that Elise stopped and turned to Hilda. "Tell me now, before Peder and Kristian can hear us."

"I've talked to the *verksmester*, Herr Paulsen."

Elise's mouth dropped. "Were you furious with him?"

Hilda laughed with a twinkle in her eye, "Are you crazy? I was with him, in his office. We were alone and I told him what had happened."

Elise glared at her sister not comprehending a word of what she was saying.

Hilda laughed again. "He told me not to worry; he'll take care of everything."

"Take care of everything?" Elise looked at her, wrinkled her brow in confusion.

"No, it's not what you think!" Hilda impatiently threw up her hands. "He doesn't want anything to happen to me. I can keep on working at the spinning mill and when *that* day comes he said I can just put my destiny in God's hands and he'll take care of the rest."

"You mean he'll pay for it?"

Hilda shrugged her shoulders, irritated. "Do I have to spoon feed you everything?!"

Elise turned away and continued up the steps. Something isn't quite right, she thought. The *verksmester* wasn't a charitable person. It was a miracle that he had even admitted to having something to do with Hilda's 'condition.' But what was he planning to do about it.....?

They were all the way to the third floor when Elise turned to Hilda again. "I think you're lying to me, Hilda."

Hilda was red in her face. "Lying?"

"Yes, I don't think you're as innocent in all of this as you want me to believe. If you were, you wouldn't have gone to the *verksmester* and been so calm. You would have chewed him out, yelling and screaming.

Hilda's eyes narrowed and she looked straight into Elise's eyes. "And what would that have helped?"

"Nothing at all."

"So why did you say such a thing?"

"Because I think you knew full well what you were doing, hoping to come away from living here in Sandakerveien."

To her surprise, Hilda looked away, marched past her and opened the door without answering. Elise had talked without weighing her words.

When she saw Hilda's reaction, she thought she might have been right. Hilda had voluntarily - at least almost voluntarily - gone to bed with the old middle aged, *verksmester*.

She was just sixteen years old! How could she? Wasn't she in love with Lorang, the errand boy? Did she really believe she would be happier with a few more *kroner* in wages, or the gifts she might get from the *verksmester*? And Mamma, such an honest and decent person, who had taught them Bible verses, sent them to Sunday School at the Salvation Army and brought them up to be proper, and God-fearing. If she didn't die from tuberculosis, *this* would be the death of her!

Elise hurried into the kitchen, sputtering to her sister, "God help you if you tell this to Mamma!"

As she put the coffee kettle on the stove and found the sugar and milk, her thoughts shifted from outrage to incomprehension. What was it with Hilda?

After Hilda had been with Mamma, Elise went in the *kammers* and looked at herself in the little mirror hanging over the dresser. What she saw was a face similar to her sister's, thin and pale with freckles and a turned-up nose. Quite average. Kinda boring, she thought and made faces at herself. If only she had Hilda's beautiful blonde hair.

But then she smiled, and her dimples brightened up her face. That must be what attracted the *verksmester's* attention...the dimples and the blonde hair...that's why he had chosen Hilda.

Her own hair wasn't that bad. Even if the brown color was boring, it was thick and long. If only she could wash it more often, but she couldn't heat up water other than for Saturday baths, it took too much wood. Besides, she always braided her hair or wore it in a bun on the top of her head to keep it out of the machines. She used a *skaut* when she walked to and from work. When she and Johan were together they were either in the dark stairwell or it was dark. There wasn't much point in trying to look glamorous when you couldn't see more than the outlines of people.

The big question was, had the *verksmester* forced himself on Hilda, or had she voluntarily gone to bed with him? Actually it didn't make any difference. It was a shame and an accident no matter what. But what did it mean that "he would take care of the rest?" Was he willing to support them? Even if the workers along Akerselva didn't care if you were pregnant and not married, she had heard it was different among the rich people.

"I have a few *kroner* in my money box."

Elise turned with surprise towards the weak voice in the bed behind her. Mamma lay there looking at her, worry in her eyes. "For material for a dress," she whispered.

Elise understood. Mamma had thought she was looking at herself in the mirror because she was thinking of the wedding. She blushed. "It's no hurry," she mumbled. "It won't be at least until summer."

When she went back into the kitchen, she found flour and milk to make *grøt*. When she could afford it, she made the *grøt* with milk for her brothers. They were growing boys and needed it.

Hilda was helping Peder with his school lesson. He used his pointer finger to read every letter in the words, and it was slow going. Sometimes he mixed up the letters and said the first letters last. Elise thought his heart was bigger and better than his reading abilities. If he could just finish school, maybe he could become a minister? But ministers had to know how to read and write otherwise there wouldn't be any sermons from the pulpit.

Kristian was the complete opposite. He had learned to read before he started school, had a good head on his shoulders and remembered what he had read. But something about Kristian worried her. He had been like this ever since he was small. All of a sudden, with no warning, he would pinch her arm or leg so hard that it hurt, and he would look at her with a hard dark look. He pulled his brother's hair or pinched his ears when he thought no one was looking, and he looked so innocent when Peder started screaming. He swore he had done nothing wrong. She had often thought Kristian had an evil streak.

But it was still Peder who got the most scolding from the teacher. He often brought home notes in his curled up little report book, saying he had done something wrong. But when Elise asked if the notes were true, he clenched his lips tightly and refused to answer. Twice she had noticed Kristian standing behind her making ugly faces at Peder.

She felt hurt for Peder. In school, the pupils who raised their hands with the right answers always got to sit up front. They were smart and knew the answers. The "dummies" were placed furthest back. Peder was one of them, but he wasn't one who didn't care. He wanted to do better. He'd told her about some pupils who threw spitballs around the room and whispered the wrong answers to them. They hid detective books like Nick Carter, Nat Pinkerton, Sherlock Holmes and Percy Stuart and comic books in their desks and read them when the teacher wasn't looking. One teacher was nicknamed "The Ruler" because he reprimanded the pupils by hitting them with a ruler or giving them a sharp flick on the ear before sending them to stand in the dunce-corner. Peder didn't dare to sneak-read and didn't have comic books, but he was rapped on the knuckles with the ruler or hit with the blackboard pointer stick because he didn't know the answers to the teacher's questions.

A careful knock on the door, and Johan stuck his head in. "It's Saturday tomorrow, Elise. Would you like to come with me to "The Pearl?"

Elise looked at him in surprise and blushed. "Can you afford that?"

"I should be able to go dancing with my favorite girl on a Saturday night," he said, sounding a little upset.

Elise regretted she'd said that. "Of course, I'll go with you, Johan. Would you like to come in?"

He took off his *skyggelua* and came into the kitchen. The room seemed smaller now when he stood there with his broad shoulders and big workman's hands. "How's it going, Peder?" he asked as he glanced towards the kitchen table where the boys were doing their school lessons. "When are you going to read to me?"

Peder didn't smile. "Hilda says I'm t'ick in my head."

"That's just because she's your sister. Girls always have to pretend they are better than us." He winked at Elise and she couldn't help but laugh.

Hilda stood up unexpectedly from the table. "Fine, you take over then!" she snapped angrily, grabbed her wool shawl and knit scarf from the hook on the wall and marched out the door.

With a puzzled look, Johan watched her leave. "What's wrong with her?" he asked when the door slammed so hard that the tin plates rattled in the dish rack hanging on the wall.

Elise shrugged her shoulders. "She hasn't been herself lately."

Kristian looked up from his arithmetic book. "I know why!"

Elise sent him a disgruntled glance. "No you don't. Hilda's not feeling well," she added quickly. "She's coughing, has a fever and really, she should be in bed."

"That's what I meant!" Kristian gave her a dirty look. "What else did'ya think I meant?"

Elise turned towards the cookstove, afraid of saying too much. "You want a *kaffesvett*, Johan?"

"Ja, please."

She set the coffee cup on the table in front of him, poured in a little milk and turned away quickly, pretending to be

79

looking for the sugar. She knew he had to be wondering. Hilda shouldn't be going out in the cold weather, not with a cough and fever.

Sooner or later she would tell Johan what had happened, but not quite yet. Not before she knew what they were going to do about it. And what the *verksmester* had decided.

Johan was so honest and respectable, so good in every way. When he found out the truth about Hilda, that she had possibly gone to bed with the *verksmester* voluntarily, maybe he would think Elise was just as bad. Maybe he would have second thoughts, and not want to marry her after all.

She poured weak coffee with milk in a cup for herself and sat down in Hilda's place at the table. "Do you know if there will be many others at "the Pearl" tomorrow?

"Wow! Ja! It'll be packed-full!! It's not every Saturday night there's a dance there!"

"I'm not sure what I'll wear…"

"Don't worry about it. The others don't have anything else to wear, either."

"So, Kristian?" He turned to her brother. "Aren't you going to start delivering newspapers soon? Or get a job as an errand boy? I've heard you're real good in school, and think you can find time for your school lessons even if you get a little job."

Kristian sent him a disgusted look, clamped his lips together and stared down at his arithmetic book without answering.

Peder looked up at Johan with kindness and innocence in his eyes. "I can ask… If ya t'nk dat can help Elise."

Johan ruffled his hair. "I think you have to be a year or two older first, Peder."

Peder looked disappointed. "Evert ain't much older 'an me."

"But he's not going to school, is he?"

Peder looked down at the page, put his pointer finger on the first letter in the word, and started to spell: "Paaappa reeeads thhhe neeewspaaaper. Maaamaa iiss bbaaakiiing bread."

"Just listen to him," Kristian said mockingly. "He can't even read a first grade book."

"Kristian!" Elise sent him a lightning flash glance. "Peder might not be as tall or as strong as you, but he has a heart that's much bigger. And he won't read any better when you're teasing him! But no matter, boys, its bedtime. You have to get up early and you need your sleep."

Both got up obediently. They knew that tone in her voice; they knew when enough was enough.

"I gotta go down to the outhouse. I'll race ya!" Kristian shouted and rushed to the door, Peder right behind him.

Johan smiled and winked at Elise. "Come sit with me a few minutes while we've got the chance."

She snuggled close to him. The next moment she felt his lips on hers.

When they finally managed to pull themselves apart, he whispered in her ear, "I've been to see the minister. I ran out during lunch break."

Elise looked at him, wide eyed. "What did he say?"

"All we have to do is decide on a date. I did say that a spring wedding would be best. No later than *St. Hansaften*, in Sagene kirke, our beautiful new church."

Her thoughts returned quickly to Hilda. If the *verksmester* was really "going to take care of everything," Elise had nothing to worry about, did she?

She leaned into his broad chest and whispered very softly, almost inaudible, "Hilda's going to have a baby."

Johan sat up abruptly. "What did you say?"

She lifted her face and looked into his eyes. "Hilda's pregnant, but you can't tell a living soul. Not yet. I don't even know if I'm allowed to say who the father is."

"Isn't it Lorang?" He looked at her questioning, his eye brows raised. "Hilda, she's only sixteen years old?"

She nodded seriously. "Mamma doesn't know yet. Neither do Peder and Kristian. I didn't even know until yesterday."

Johan seemed very upset, and normally he was the calm one. "Are you sure?!"

"No, we can't be, not for a while yet, but...but..." Elise shrugged her shoulders helplessly. "But it looks like she could be."

Johan sighed heavily. "Let's just hope she can keep her job, even if she has to quit awhile when her stomach gets big."

Elise nodded. She wanted to tell him it looked like Hilda would be able to continue working in the mill, but didn't want to say anything yet. Not before Hilda told her it was ok.

He sat there staring thoughtfully into the air, as if he'd had the wind knocked out of him. "Can you imagine..." he mumbled. "Only sixteen..."

"Don't think about it, Johan. I'm sure it'll work out okay." She sat quietly before whispering excitedly, "I told Mamma you proposed to me. She told me to say yes!"

Johan smiled, hugged her tightly and found her lips again.

They didn't let go of each other until they heard the boys coming up the steps. Elise hurriedly got off his lap and moved to the other stool. "Johan?" she whispered quickly before Peder and Kristian came in, "did you turn it in?"

For a moment he looked quizzically at her, not knowing what she was talking about. Then he nodded. "Everything has been taken care of, Elise, you can forget about it."

"Did you go to the police or to the director? What did he say? Was it his daughter's?"

"Ja...well, it wasn't really hers, but he recognized it. Don't think any more about it," he repeated.

He stood up. "I have to go down again. Anna's not feeling so good today."

"Say hello to her from me. Tell her I'll drop by tomorrow evening."

He nodded and left just as Peder and Kristian came storming into the kitchen.

"There was a huge rat by the outhouse door," Kristian shouted. "I tried to get him, but Peder scared him away."

"Kristian woud 'ave stamped on 'im 'til he died," Peder said, concern in his voice. "Dat ain't right, is it, Elise?"

"No, he can't do that," Elise answered, but her thoughts were in a completely different place.

"I could'a killed him with the axe," Kristian shot back. "If ya hadn't chased him away."

"Shhh boys, you've got to be quiet for Mamma."

They calmed down, got undressed and went quietly into the *kammers*.

"*Natta*, Elise."

"*Natta*, Peder. *Natta*, Kristian."

Elise dumped the dishwater into the scrub bucket, drizzled in a drop of ammonia and went out in the dark stairwell to scrub the steps. Her body ached from exhaustion. When Johan became a foreman, and he would soon, he would earn at least two *kroner* more per week. Then they could afford their own small place. Maybe, they'd have their own little kitchen that they wouldn't have to share with another family. It would be a complete little apartment. She would make it so cozy\, with plants in the windowsills, a freshly starched tablecloth on the kitchen table and crisp, white curtains in the windows.

Or even better, maybe a small, painted red house just like the one down by the bridge, belonging to the old man who owned the spinning mill. It would have a porch warmed by sunshine in the summer, a fireplace in the kitchen, a small living room with a plush sofa, a shiny, polished table, and a steep staircase to the *kammers* in the attic. Warm summer Saturday and Sunday evenings they would sit out on the porch and listen to the whispering river, birds twittering in the big oak trees and happy childrens' voices coming from the grassy meadows below. Johan and she, just the two of them, and soft summer evenings. Thank you, God - what happiness...

And now she was rid of that pesky brooch for good. The director had taken it without interrogating questions; otherwise, Johan would have told her. Good, kind Johan....

Chapter 7

The weather had turned milder, old snow under foot had turned to slush and a heavy mixture of snow and rain was falling in the air.

Elise and Johan walked arm in arm, her arm tucked into his. It felt strange, showing the whole world they belonged together. She had mixed feelings, both proud and shy at the same time.

"Do you hear it?" She stopped and listened, filled with excitement. "Do you hear the music?!"

Johan nodded. They passed under a gas lamp and the dim light fell on his face.

She looked up at him. She loved him so much it hurt. "I'm no good at dancing."

He laughed and put her arms around him. "Do you think I'm any better?"

Then he wrapped his arms around her and drew her closer. "Elise, we don't have to dance." he whispered. "We can just stand close together swaying to the music, while the others dance past us."

She giggled, just wanting to feel his arms around her. "What if someone sees us?" she whispered nervously.

"So what? Can't they handle seeing a couple in love?"

She could do nothing but laugh.

They continued their stroll down the street. The music grew louder the closer they got, the air filled with both apprehension and excitement.

Then Elise heard someone call her name. She turned and saw Agnes and three other girls, arm in arm, laughing and giggling. She was sure they were on their way to "The Pearl," too.

Elise hadn't seen Agnes in several days. Agnes didn't work at the spinning mill, but at the Hjula Weaving Mill, the next factory over. Before they had usually spent their evenings together after all their chores were done, but since she and Johan were spending more time together, it was seldom. It bothered her a bit. She felt as if she had deserted her best friend.

"Are ya goin' to "The Pearl?" Agnes called out.

Elise nodded. Suddenly she felt embarrassed, standing arm in arm with Johan, like an old married couple, but, when she tried to pull her arm away he held on tightly. "You're going, too?"

The girls nodded, gazing first at Johan, then at her, and back to Johan. Envy was written all over their faces.

"I saw Hilda going across the bridge. If she's left something at the mill, it ain't open now," one of them burst out.

"I know. That's not where she was going," Elise said.

The girl laughed. "She got herself a boyfriend on t' wrong side of the river?"

Elise nodded and laughed.

"Come on, Agnes," the other girls harassed. "Can't ya see they're lettin' people in?"

Elise and Johan stood back and let the girls go ahead of them. As soon as they were out of earshot Johan turned and faced her. "What was all that talk about Hilda? Is it true?"

Elise bit her lip. "Just something I came up with," she mumbled.

"You don't know why she was going over the bridge?"

She shook her head. "No, but I have a feeling someone is over there."

"The father of the baby, you mean?"

She nodded; glad they weren't standing under a gas lamp. If he'd seen her face, he would know she had lied.

They'd reached "The Pearl." There was a line of people waiting to get into the dance hall. The music was thundering, and couple after couple swirled past them, the dance had started. In the room next door tables and chairs were placed on the edge of the dance floor. Behind the bar was "Ruski," a big Russian with a dark mustache, red rounded-cheeks and a big beer belly. He had signed off from a Russian cargo ship in Kristiania over twenty years ago, had started with nothing and now he owned "The Pearl" and even a small house in Sagveien.

"Would you like a beer, or would you rather dance?" Johan looked at her, a happy glint in his blue eyes.

She smiled. "What do you want?

He laughed. "I asked first."

"Then I'd rather dance."

His arm around her back, he escorted her to the dance floor, as if it were the most natural thing in the world.

Ever since she was a little girl Elise had loved music. Her mother had told her she'd been singing, in tune, since she was two years old. She had never taken dance lessons, but she had rhythm and learned quickly by watching others. She wasn't afraid of doing the wrong dance step, like many others she'd seen.

Johan put his cheek to hers and held her close. She felt like she was floating on air. She closed her eyes and thought she could dance like this with Johan, cheek to cheek, forever, until the end of time. She couldn't wish for anything more in the world than to come again to "The Pearl" and dance with Johan.

After they'd danced one dance after another Johan slipped his hand into hers. "I'm thirsty, let's take a break and get a beer."

Nearly all the tables in the other room were taken. The room was filled with talk and laughter mixed with the clanking of beer bottles, swearing, coughing and spitting. Lots of the guys used chewing tobacco. Every now and then the spittoons "sang." Agnes had said it made them manlier. But Elise was happy that Johan didn't chew. The smell was rancid and rotten, like a sour old shoe sole.

They went all the way to the back table. Johan sat down and pulled her onto his lap. Smoke hung like a heavy blanket of fog under the low ceiling. A couple of kerosene lamps hung from the beams in the ceiling and sent weak streams of light around the room. The corners were dimly lit.

"So Johan, dat your gal?" a loud boisterous voice shouted from the other side of the room. "By gosh, you be'n lucky!"

Johan smiled, raised his beer bottle towards the man and shouted *skål.* Then he took a couple of swigs before offering Elise a drink.

Just then they heard a terrible commotion in the doorway, and two drunks came staggering in, each with a girl on his arm. Elise could see from their clothes and their behavior that they were street-girls. One of them, especially, caught her eye. She had such a strange smile, a smile that Elise had never seen the likes of before. She thought she looked like someone who had died with a stiff smile on her lips and she'd never be able to close her mouth again. She was dirty, wore ragged clothes, was half-drunk and had a strange blue color under her eyes.

Both men were up in years. One had a *skyggelua* pulled far down over his on forehead, a dirty long beard, and messy clothes with a filthy vest missing every other button. Elise thought something was oddly familiar about him, but couldn't see him properly in the dim light and all the smoke.

The four stumbled towards a table that had just been vacated. The man with the *skyggelua* pulled it off and Elise immediately felt a sharp pain shoot through her whole being. Her face turned deep red with shame. She wanted to turn and look the other way, but couldn't. Unable to move, Elise glared at her father and the street-girl sitting on his lap. Her heart pounded as frightful rage built up. At home Mamma lay in bed, sick and miserable; unable to do anything and only living off what Elise and Hilda managed to scrounge together. And here he sat, obviously drunk on expensive booze before coming here and already three sheets to the wind, beer on the table and a street-girl on his lap, who most likely demanded both beer and shiny coins for the services she willingly sold.

Johan also saw who he was. "Do you want to leave, Elise?" he looked at her with sympathy.

She nodded, got up, and forced herself to march past the table where the four of them were sitting. She avoided looking at them and ran out of the tavern.

When they were outside, she breathed in short heavy gasps, her body shaking like a leaf.

"That miserable bum!" Tears streamed down her face. "Spending his money on other women when Mamma is laying sick in bed at home." She sobbed, bit her lips trying to hold the tears back, but couldn't.

Johan put his arms around her. "Come, let's go. We can't leave Peder and Kristian alone with your mother much longer anyway. We danced a little, saw some night life, tasted the beer and know what it's all about. We're better off at home, Elise."

He held her hand as they walked side-by-side while big, wet snowflakes filled the air. The snowflakes lay like a white carpet over dirty roads and drains, over rusty water posts, and stinky garbage cans in dark backyards.

"Forget it, Elise. He's not worthy of your tears. You know how he is, this isn't the first time. Your mother knows, too. It's been a long time since you were standing by the window, waiting and watching for him. I'm sure you all have it better when he's not at home. Have you forgotten how it was? All those times you were beaten. And your mother, too."

She shook her head and dried her tears with her knit scarf. "He's so low-down rotten. He knows Mamma is sick. He knows she couldn't work the whole last year. What does he think we're all living on?"

"He doesn't think. He's only doing like everyone else who has lost his job and can't face the reality of poverty. We can't help how we're created, Elise. Some are born with strength and willpower, others are not. And now the alcohol has taken over."

"You're so thoughtful and understanding, Johan. I love you."

"And I love you."

The gas lamp by the gate was broken. They stood quietly together in the dark corner, their arms wrapped around each other, without saying a word. The tearful lump in her throat was gone and now she wished she could just stand like this with Johan, all night long, even if her toes were freezing.

"Go up to bed, Elise, so you don't get sick. If Hilda's home tomorrow, maybe we can take a stroll downtown," he added eagerly. "We can walk up Karl Johansgate; look at all the lights, the shop windows, and the sleighs going by. It's still Christmas you know. Well, at least for some."

Elise smiled in the dark. "I'm looking forward to it."

They said their goodbyes outside his door. It felt like her heart was in her throat when she went up to the third floor. She tried to tell herself that as long as there was life, there was hope. She still had her mother, and miracles had happened before and could happen again. There was no use in dreading the future, it would come whether one wanted it to or not.

Still, she felt the same fear every time she opened the door to the little *kammers*.

"Mamma? Are you sleeping?"

"No need to whisper, Elise." Her mother's voice was surprisingly awake and clear.

Elise hurried in. Peder and Kristian were sound asleep. "I wasn't gone too long, was I?"

Mamma smiled in the flickering light from the candle on the dresser. "I didn't think you'd be home for quite a while yet. "Did you have a good time?"

Elise was amazed. Her mother hadn't spoken that much in ages. Could there really still be hope?

"Ja. We danced!"

Her mother smiled again and looked at her. "I'm sure you learned quickly, you have always been good with music."

"Am I musical?"

Her mother nodded. "You could sing perfectly since you were two years old."

"I've heard you say that before, but I didn't think it meant much."

Her mother nodded seriously. "If you had been born on the other side of the river, Elise, you would have made something of yourself."

Elise giggled shyly. "Now you're kidding. Are you feeling a little better tonight, Mamma?"

Her mother nodded. "It has been so strange. All of a sudden I could breathe easier and I'm not as dead tired like I've been the last few days. I have been feeling so heavy, like I could sink right through the floor."

Elise looked at her, amazed, and then she looked over at her brothers. "Did they do as I asked and make supper and weak coffee for you?"

"Yes, they've been like two little angels."

Elise had trouble picturing Kristian as an angel, but didn't say anything. "And Hilda?"

"I told her she could stay out until ten o'clock."

Elise didn't ask where her sister was. "I'll have some bread before I go to bed."

"Do that, Elise. Hilda is so grownup and sensible, she'll take care of herself."

That's what you think, Elise thought with a sigh, as she went out to the kitchen. What will Mamma say the day she hears the truth......

Chapter 8

Elise awoke abruptly! What in the world was going on?! She sat up in bed and listened. Then she heard it again, boisterous loud voices coming from the kitchen.

Had Hilda brought someone home with her? Elise glanced over at the window. It was pitch dark outside so it had to be in the middle of the night. She held her breath and listened. Men's voices...Oh Lord, what was Hilda up to?

No way would she have brought Herr Paulsen, *verksmester*, up here!

She heard clinking of bottles, laughing and loud racket. A woman's voice burst out, but it wasn't Hilda's. How many were out there? Elise felt anger building. Why in the world had Hilda brought her friends home in the middle of the night? There was nothing here for them, and Mamma, Peder and Kristian were sleeping. Had Hilda completely lost her mind? She was pregnant and not feeling well.

Then came a new another roar of laughter. Elise sprang out of bed, irritated, as her barefeet hit the cold wooden floor planks. In the dark, she fumbled to the hook on the wall, took down her wool shawl, threw it around her shoulders and opened the door.

Two men and two women were sitting around the kitchen table, the same four she had seen at "The Pearl." One of the girls was on her father's lap, her blouse undone and her breasts hanging halfway out.

"Yep, dat's my lil'l girl," her father slurred. "Come 'ere, Elise, and say hi to m' gal. Ain't she fine?" And with his dirty hand he grabbed her white breasts. As the woman snickered with delight, stubs of brown rotten teeth showed themselves.

Elise took a deep breath, closed the *kammers* door behind her. Her heart beating so hard that she thought it would explode. "Get out! Mamma is sick!" she shrieked at them.

"Good grief, wha's got inta ya?"

"Mamma is sick! She can't tolerate all this commotion. Besides, she's still your wife, in case you've forgotten!"

Pappa gave the street-girl a hard shove that sent her flying to the floor. He grappled and got up on his unsteady legs, sneering at Else with an evil glint. "Dammit, ya got a mouth on ya! How dare ya talk to you' ol' man like that? To hell with ya! Ya need ta learn a t'ing or two. If ya t'ink ya can chase ya' ol man 'way from his own house, ya gotta another t'ing comin'."

Elise stood frozen watching her father stagger towards her. No way did she want Mamma to wake to this noisy row. She'd rather stand her ground and fight him.

Then his hand flew forward and hit her across her nose and mouth. The pain cut through her. She could taste the sweet taste of blood. She had tasted it before.

"Do ya hear me?" He yelled. "I ain't leavin' my own damn kitchen!"

"*Your* kitchen?" Elise was explosive with anger. "And what have you contributed, if I may ask?"

The next hit came with a closed fist. Stars danced in front of her eyes, she wobbled and fell back against the wall.

In a flash, the door flew open, and in the middle of the door stood Johan, fully dressed, looking like he'd been caught in a thunder storm. He immediately grasped the situation, charged in, grabbed Pappa and dragged him away. The other man got up from the kitchen table, amazingly light on his feet. He swung at Johan, and soon the three of them were thrashing around on the floor and rolled out the door. Elise caught glimpses of flying fists and fresh blood, and heard swear words echoing in the dark stairwell. The two street-girls jumped up, sneaked their way past the fight and escaped down the steps.

Elise stood watching, shaking from both the cold and fright, afraid of the outcome. It was two against one, but two of them were drunk, and Johan was strong.

"Go inside, Elise!" Johan shouted in the middle of the turmoil. "Close the door so your mother doesn't hear the ruckus."

She did as he said; there wasn't much else she could do. Sobbing and trembling, overcome with pain and anger, she stood in the middle of the kitchen until she heard the swearing, shouting and spectacle disappear down the steps. Now she was afraid the tenement manager would come storming out of his door on the first floor, and evict them from their home immediately.

Finally, it was quiet. And in minutes she heard footsteps in the stairwell. Johan stuck his head in the door. His nose was bleeding, his *busserullen* was torn to shreds and his pants were covered in mud.

Johan looked at her. "Are you okay?"

She nodded with a sob. "I was so scared for Mamma."

He came inside. "Have you heard any sounds from the *kammers*?"

She shook her head, found a rag, dipped it in cold water and placed it over his bloody nose.

Johan put his arms around her. "Don't cry, Elise. I don't think he'll dare come back. Not for a quite awhile."

She relaxed in the warmth of his arms; feeling ashamed and yet thinking she should be used to this. It wasn't the first time Pappa had come home drunk and belligerent. It wasn't the first time he had dragged women home with him, either.

"Go down and get some sleep, Johan. Your mother and Anna are no doubt concerned about you."

Reluctantly he let her go, gently stroked her cheek and left. Elise held her breath as she returned quietly to the *kammers*. Was Mamma awake? Had she understood what had happened?

In the dark, she groped her way to her straw mattress on the floor.

"Elise?" It was Peder's voice, he sounded scared. "Is 'e still 'ere?"

"No, they've gone. Go back to sleep."

"Why did dey make so terrible much noise?"

"Because they'd drunk too much moonshine."

"Where'd 'e get the money from?"

"From the Poorhouse, maybe. I don't know. Go to sleep, Peder."

"Where's 'e sleepin'? Pappa, I mean?"

"I don't know."

"Maybe dem at da Salvation Army helps 'im?" There was hope in his voice.

"I'm sure they do. Go back to sleep."

She heard a weak cough from Mamma's bed. Elise was sure she was awake. It wasn't possible to have slept through that noisy commotion.

Inspite of being so worked-up, sleep took over as soon as her head hit the pillow.

She woke with a start and saw to her dismay it was already daylight outside. The factory sirens must have blown a long time ago. Filled with dread, she got up from her mattress. Then with relief, she suddenly realized it was Sunday! She sank back down on her mattress, but immediately was startled again. Hilda's bed was empty....

She hadn't given any thought to Hilda until now, had taken it for granted that she was asleep in her bed. Hilda was a sound sleeper. She could sleep through anything, even Pappa at his worst.

Elise glanced over at Mamma's bed; she seemed to be sleeping restfully. Peder and Kristian were still asleep, too, laying head to foot in their narrow bed. Quietly she rose, rushed over the cold wooden plank floor to the kitchen. Shivering, she built a fire in the woodstove, splashed a drop of ice cold water on her face and dressed in a hurry. She'd taken her Saturday bath before she went out with Johan last evening and still felt clean. She didn't need to wash so much today.

The wind howled in the chimney. It must have started blowing hard again. The temperature must also have dropped since it was so freezing cold in the kitchen. She rubbed her hands together over the woodstove, blew warm breath into them and slapped her shoulders to keep warm. Then ladled cold water into the coffee kettle, pulled the smaller rings out of the set of iron rings on the top of the woodstove, and set the coffee kettle in the opening to cook the water as quickly as possible. She deserved to sit down and treat herself to a strong cup of coffee today - with sugar and milk. It was Sunday, after all!

She'd have to lie to Mamma. She couldn't tell her Hilda had been gone all night. It was bad enough that Pappa had been here again, sloppy drunk and had dragged along women and a drinking buddy.

That Hilda could show so little respect and stay out all night when Mamma was so sick. She'd promised to be home by ten o'clock. That new girlfriend she'd found was apparently not a good decent girl. She lived in a tiny attic room in that old wooden frame house down by Seilduken and didn't have anyone to look after her. She was from a *husmannsplass* up by Lake Mjøsa, the biggest lake in Norway, and had come alone to Kristiania, when she was fifteen years old.

There, finally, she heard the sound of feet coming up the steps. Hilda no doubt had a bad conscience now and deserved it. She should feel shame. Elise threw an irritated glance toward the door.

The footsteps came nearer, slower and with caution. Now she's getting panicky, I can hear it, Elise thought.

To her astonishment, there was a knock on the door and it was carefully opened. In the opening stood an out-of-breath Fru Evertsen. "There's a dead body layin' down by the bridge." Her voice was trembling. "They say it's one who drowned 'imself. I had to find out if you were all 'ere."

Hilda…Elise thought immediately as a jolt of fear shot through her.

Chapter 9

Elise legs trembled when she stood up and stumbled towards Fru Evertsen grabbing onto her arm. She needed to know! She tried to speak, but couldn't open her mouth. "Did you see if it was…" in a strained voice when the words finally came out. "I mean…"

Fru Evertsen shook her head. "Dere was so many folk standin' 'round dere. I yust 'eard 'em say 'e done it on purpose. It ain't da first time," she added. "And in dat freezin' cold river water…"

Elise stood quietly, paralyzed with anxiety. Hilda hadn't been home all night. She hadn't seen her since she sputtered to her that she mustn't tell Mamma. Maybe Hilda had finally realized the hopelessness of her situation and had done the same as other girls before her…

Fru Evertsen turned to leave. "I yust 'ad to know dat nobody's missin', but I see everythin's all right 'ere."

Elise fumbled for words. "Was it…? Did you see if it was…?"

"How would I know, w'en I couldn't even see who it was? Oh, Lord, what a awful way to die. Maybe it was a bum, din't have a place to live. Maybe 'e was so cold and froze so 'ard, dat 'e din't see where 'e was walkin'? Or maybe it was a young girl who'd got 'erself in trouble and din't know any other way…?"

"But, but didn't you see…," Elise was desperate, "didn't you get even one tiny, little glimpse?!"

Fru Evertsen shook her head. "All I saw was a bunch of nosey women crowded over somethin'. Ya'd t'ink dey was at the circus, shovin' and pushin' to get in da front line." She sighed loudly, "I 'member what Signe did... It's maybe yust as good dat dey put an end to it..."

Elise had to support herself against the wall. It couldn't be Hilda, she told herself. One of Agnes' girlfriends had seen Hilda going over the bridge last night. Friday night she had been happy and had said the *verksmester* would help her.

But Elise had been furious with her and shrieked that she would be sorry if she told Mamma.

Oh, Lord. Maybe she'd found out the *verksmester* wouldn't help her after all? Lord, my God, what has Hilda gotten herself into.....?

On the verge of fainting, she closed her eyes, nauseated and overcome with panic as thoughts flashed through her mind about what would happen. It'll be the death of Mamma. Peder will mope with sorrow and Kristian will be even more somber and withdrawn. They would only have her wages to live on and she would have lost her only sister and no longer have anyone to share her sorrows and worries with. She would come home alone during the lunch break, no one to sit at the kitchen table with, no one to help with Mamma, help with washing clothes, darning stockings and patching Peder's and Kristian's pants. No one she could laugh and giggle with, nor gossip about the other girls at the spinning mill.

"Whad's wrong wid ya?" Fru Evertsen turned toward her. She hadn't noticed Elise's reaction until now.

"Nothing." She shook her head. "It's just terrible to think about. That freezing slush," she added and took a deep breath.

Fru Evertsen nodded. "Don't let da accident affect ya so." She took a couple of steps. "Let's yust hope it ain't one we know," she added with a heavy sigh. "It's worse when ya know 'em."

She turned to Elise again. "How's Hilda nowadays? I t'ink she looks pale and skinny. Nothin' wrong wid her, is der?"

Elise shook her head quickly, overcome with fear, swallowing hard to hold back the tears. "Not that I know of. Well, I mean, she says she's always freezing, but doesn't everybody this time of the year?"

She thought Fru Evertsen gave her a strange look, but didn't know if she was imagining it.

Fru Evertsen took another couple of steps toward the door. "I 'ave to get downstairs again. I'll let ya know if I 'ear sumthin'." With that she waddled out of the kitchen.

Elise stood frozen on the spot, her body shaking in fear. Fru Evertsen's words came back and rang in her ears, "I 'member what Signe did... Maybe its best dey put an end to everythin'..."

She put her hand over her mouth to keep from crying out loud. Her fingers were ice cold. "No, no!" she whispered under her breath.

Thoughts tumbled and raced in her head. Words that had been exchanged, looks she had noticed. Was there something she should have done differently? Had she been too strict with Hilda? Maybe she should have cried with her instead of scolding her.

Maybe it was too late now...

She covered her face with her hands and sobbed quietly, her whole body shaking.

"Dear God, please don't let it be her," she begged. "Please, let Hilda be alive. I'm begging you with all my heart, please."

Then she heard heavy footsteps coming up the steps. Elise stared at the door, her instincts were becoming reality.

She held her breath, heard the knock on the door and knew what was going to happen even before the door opened.

"Come in!" Her voice was weak.

The door opened and on the threshold stood two constables, with their spiked helmets, mustaches and shiny buttons on their uniforms. Elise gasped. So, she had been right. It *was* Hilda who lay stiff and frozen in the icy river. Hilda had chosen to die instead of having the baby and living with the shame; even if Herr Paulsen had said he would help her.

"Marlene Løvlien?" said one of them with a rough, brusque voice.

"She...she's in there." Elise pointed toward the *kammers*, her teeth chattering. "She's sick."

"And you are?" The constable gave her a curious look.

"Her daughter," she replied, a lump of anxiety and fear in her throat. For a brief second she thought maybe they were going door to door, talking with everyone in the area so it wasn't Hilda after all, but deep down she knew the worst. Fru Evertsen's words still rang in her ears: "Or maybe it was a young girl who'd got 'erself in trouble and din't know any other way..."?

The constable took a deep breath. "We are bringing you bad news, I'm afraid. A man has fallen in the river and drowned, and there are indications it's your father."

Elise put both hands over her mouth and looked at the constable, trying to comprehend what he had said. It wasn't Hilda! She felt unbelievable relief. She wanted to laugh and cry at the same time. Then reality struck. It was Pappa who was dead! It was *he* who had thrown himself in the foaming, icy water, or slid on the ice and had fallen in without anyone to rescue him. Frenzied thoughts raced through her head.

She burst into tears, not knowing if it was for Pappa or that she was so relieved it wasn't Hilda after all. She was trembling again, shaking so hard that her teeth chattered. Not because Pappa was dead, she had wished that on him many a time, but because she suddenly remembered all that had happened last night, when he'd been shoved out the door into the frost laden night. She'd locked him out in the cold of winter; drunk and shabbily dressed, without he himself knowing how dangerous it was. Either he'd intentionally slid under the rusty railing, or he had slipped on the ice. She didn't know which was worse.

"Sad news for you, Miss, even if he hadn't lived at home the last couple years," the other constable seemed uneasy. "Ja, he was one of those; we knew him. You're so pale. Should I get the doctor?"

She shook her head. "No, thank you. It came so..." She shook her head and tried to stop crying. "What happened? I mean, did he slip on the ice, or...?" She raised a hand to her mouth, not wanting to show how afraid she was to hear the answer and thinking how strange she was probably acting.

"We don't know yet, but the bridge was icy. It was snowing heavily. And..." He shrugged his shoulders, stopped there. And he was drunk, Elise finished his sentence to herself.

"I have to tell Mamma."

Now the constables were in a hurry. "You'll have to come down to the police station at Storgata 40 and identify him," one shouted over his shoulder as they were leaving. "He's in the cooler room."

After they'd gone, she stood motionless in the middle of the room, her arms crossed. She was filled with anger, regret and some sorrow. She should be relieved that the uproar he made when he came staggering home, swearing and hitting,

103

was over, but diffuse pleasant memories danced in front of her eyes and shoved the painful memories to the side. Memories from another time, actually not more than a couple years ago, but it felt like an eternity.

She knew she should go into the *kammers* and tell Mamma, but not yet. First she had to pull herself together, sort out the chaos in her head. The thought that it could have been Hilda who lay stiff and frozen by the bridge still filled her mind.

Then she heard light steps outside, the door flung open and Hilda stood in the doorway, clearly upset. "Did you hear? A drunk fell in the river last night."

Elise didn't understand. She should have thrown her arms around Hilda with relief and tearfully told her the news, but instead she was filled with rage. "That drunk was your father! Where have you been?!"

Hilda stared, her eyes wide. "Pappa?" Uncertainty in her voice. The color left her face, she turned ash-white. "How do you know?"

"Two constables just left. They asked me to come down to the police station in Storgata and identify him."

"But…how…what…? Why was he by the river under the bridge? Had he been *here*?"

Elise nodded. "Ja, he was here late last night, with another drunk and two street-girls. The worst kind." She heard the bitterness and turmoil in her voice, but couldn't stop.

Hilda bowed her head. Not in irritation, as it appeared. But more in silent and disbelieving sorrow.

Elise's anger softened. "Where have you been?" she repeated.

Hilda looked away, went to the cookstove and poured a drop of coffee. "What do you mean?"

"Mamma said you had promised to be home by ten last night, but you didn't come home. You were gone all night."

"I told you, that's none of your business!"

"Yes, it is. I'm in charge as long as Mamma is sick in bed, and you can tell that to your new girlfriend, too."

Hilda said nothing. When Elise glanced at her, she saw Hilda's face was red. Skepticism surfaced in Elise. "Isn't that where you've been?"

Hilda didn't answer.

"I asked, isn't that where you've been?" Elise grabbed her arm and shook her. Her suspicion shifted to irritation. "God help you if you get into any more trouble, Hilda! Mamma has enough to deal with right now. She doesn't need to hear that her daughter is running the streets with drunks and street-girls, ruining both herself and her reputation. And to top it all off you're pregnant!"

Hilda looked straight into Elise's eyes. "Could it occur to you that I'd be doing something else? You always think the worst."

Elise looked at her, stunned. "Something else? What do you mean?"

Hilda met her eyes, an arrogant look on her face. "Maybe I wasn't home exactly because I am pregnant."

Elise shook her head, confused. "I don't understand. What are you talking about?"

"You know whose fault this is. Maybe I was with him all night?"

"Herr Paulsen? *Verksmester?*" Elise asked in a shocked whisper.

Hilda smiled. "You're not as thick in the head as I was beginning to think."

"Isn't he married?"

"He *was*. His wife died." Hilda said with defiance in her voice.

Elise stood and gathered her thoughts. Life was one big mess, and it was falling apart! She thought about Pappa again, and Fru Evensen's words came to her like a doomsday warning: "Oh, Lord, what a awful way to die. Maybe it was a bum, din't 'ave no place to live. Maybe 'e was so cold and froze so 'ard, dat 'e din't see where 'e was walkin'."

Hilda must have understood, because her eyes softened, and tears rolled down her cheeks. "Please, Elise, don't tell Mamma what you know…about last night…and the other stuff…"

Elise looked at her. "Oh, now suddenly you think she has enough to deal with?"

Hilda lowered her head, in shame.

"I'm going in to her now. I haven't told her about Pappa…," Elise said.

Just as she was putting her hand out to open the *kammers* door, it opened silently and slowly. In the opening, appeared a pale boy's face, with huge frightened eyes.

"Peder, are you awake?"

He stood meekly in front of her, looking curiously between her and Hilda.

"You heard something?" Elise asked softly.

He didn't answer, but raised his head and looked into Elise's eyes. His eyes were like a deep, dark well. She wanted to go past him and into Mamma, but he was in the way. "Din't 'e 'ave no place to sleep?"

Elise picked him up, although he was a big boy, and hugged him tightly. He's just skin and bones, she thought, when she felt his thin body through his pajamas. "He slid on the ice, Peder. When folks stagger, sometimes they slide and fall on the ice."

"Couldn't dem at dat Sa'vation Army help 'im?" Peder asked with pain and sobbing in his voice, his body trembling.

"If he had asked, I'm sure they'd have helped him. The Salvation Army helps all those who ask. No more crying, Peder. Now Pappa is up in heaven with the angels and has it better than he's ever had it."

"How can 'e be up in heav'n wid dem angels when 'e's layin' under da bridge?"

"His body is under the bridge, but his soul is in heaven with the angels."

"I want 'im here wit'out his soul," Peder sobbed laying his head on her shoulder.

That's what we've had all along Elise thought to herself. She carried him to Mamma's bed and laid him beside her.

Mamma was awake, her eyes full of sorrow. She stroked Peder's hair with her thin, bony hand. Elise saw she had heard everything. The tears started to run down her thin, pale face as she carefully continued to stroke Peder's hair. "Now you and Kristian have to take turns being the man of the house," she said.

Elise knew Mamma wasn't grieving over the man she'd lost during the night, but the man she'd loved and lost before alcohol stole him from her.

Hilda came in. "Elise," she whispered, "Johan is in the kitchen."

Elise pulled herself together. Troubled thoughts had gnawed in her after she realized it was Pappa who'd been found dead by the river. What had happened after Johan and the two had tumbled down the steps? What had Johan done to send him away? Could the drowning have something to do with the fight?

Numb with anxiety she went quietly towards the kitchen, leaving Peder crying in Mamma's arms. Kristian wasn't in the *kammers*; he must have sneaked out when she was busy with Peder and Mamma.

"Go in to Peder and Mamma, Hilda." No anger in her voice now, one look at her sister's face was enough to forget about the other concerns. They'd deal with it later.

Hilda dried her tears and straightened her back. Actually, she wanted the best for Mamma, too.

After Hilda had disappeared through the door, Elise looked over at Johan. He stood quietly, didn't seem quite so sure of himself.

"You heard, I guess."

He nodded and twirled his *skyggelua* between his hands. "I saw them when they arrived. Mamma had already heard from Fru Evertsen. I understand she has been up here, too."

She looked at him, thinking he'd say more, but he didn't.

"How...? I mean... What happened....?"

He shook his head. "I don't know anything other than I sent him out head first."

She glanced towards the *kammers* door and lowered her voice. "Could he have been hit so hard that something happened to him? You know what I mean."

He shook his head again. "I don't know. The river isn't far but he could not have fallen because of what happened here."

She whispered. "I didn't say anything about the fight, Johan. They didn't ask. They consider this an ordinary accident. Drunkards fall all the time, and some fall in the river."

"But, you have other thoughts?" he said, a wounded look in his eyes.

"No. No, I don't, Johan. I'm feeling a mixture of sorrow and relief, but I might have been a little hard on him. I could have sent the other three on their way, after all this was still his home."

Now Johan shook his head. "You couldn't have let him keep on like that, not when your mother is so sick in bed. And I don't dare think what could have happened if I hadn't come up. We didn't have any other choice, Elise. Neither you nor I wanted anything bad to happen to him; we just wanted him to go away for a while, until he sobered up again."

They heard footsteps and women's voices out in the stairwell.

"Ah, here come all the nosey gossiping hens wanting to hear all the details." Johan was edgy. "I have to go downstairs. You know where to find me."

She nodded, thinking about what he had said. What had happened wasn't Johan's fault. Many would have done exactly the same, especially if they saw their girlfriend getting beaten.

It was Fru Evertsen, who'd no doubt seen the constables, along with Valborg's mother. Fru Evertsen came with fake sympathy plastered on her wrinkled face. Toothless, hallow cheeks, shriveled body, bent-over arthritic back, a ragged grey *skaut* tied under her chin and stubborn tangled gray hair sticking out by her ears. Valborg's mother, an even worse gossip than her daughter, crooked back, wearing dirty, worn out clothes that stunk a combination of pipe tobacco, sweat and cat-piss. She had stiff grey hairs on her chin and a huge, black wart by her nose. Mamma said that Valborg's mother had always looked that way, and Elise wondered many times what in the world Valborg's father had seen in her.

"Oh, poor you, Elise," Fru Evertsen moaned. "To think you lost your fat'er, such a friendly and gallant gentleman 'e was. I 'member once 'e carried my washed clothes up all the steps, and 'e always tipped 'is hat and said 'ello like I was a fine missus from da other side of da river."

Elise didn't remember ever seeing Pappa wearing a hat, but didn't say anything. The two of them went straight to the kitchen table and sat down, without being asked in by Elise.

"Now you gotta tell us everythin,'" Fru Evertsen went right on talking, trying to catch her breath. "Sum' says der was a ruckus 'ere last night, but I'm such a 'eavy sleeper, I never 'eard nothin' at all."

"I have to go down to the police station in Storgata and identify him," Elise said carefully. "That's what you always have to do when someone has drowned."

"Well, ya can tell us what happened, can't ya?" Fru Evertsen pursed her lips.

"I don't know anything other than what the constables told me. He was found down by the bridge, they believe he had fallen in."

"Jammen, was he *here*? How was 'e when 'e was 'ere?"

"Just like always, no different. Won't you go in and talk with Mamma?

The women blinked, their eyes roamed around the room and looked uneasily at each other.

"I was thinkin' I'd go to church an' pray for 'im," Valborg's mother mumbled.

"Me, too," Fru Evertsen said quickly and got up hurriedly from the stool, frail and feeble as she was. "Say 'ello from us. Tell 'er we'll be back once the worst is over."

Elise caught a few words as they disappeared down the steps. "I t'nk Magda on da Corner said der was two of dem street-girls wid 'im up 'ere? Dat was whad she said when I met 'er on da corner dis morning."

Elise closed the door slowly behind them. A new thought came. Anxiety flared up again. What if the two street-girls told the police that Johan had thrown Pappa out? Maybe even told them Johan had hit him so hard that he bled.

Then the police would be suspicious that it was Johan's fault...

Chapter 10

The loud ringing of church bells broke through the stillness of Sunday morning as she hurried down toward the Police Station in Storgata.

For a brief moment, she imagined walking here in the town, arm in arm with Johan, looking in the store windows and at the sleighs going by, with fur clad Christmas guests on their way to Christmas parties. The fantasy was like reading fairytales, with a princess, the trolls and Askeladden. Instead she was going to see her father for the very last time. Where he was now? In heaven?

Every time she walked past Our Saviors Church during the Christmas season, she thought about the fable "Christmas Eve from Yesteryears" and she always felt the same frightful goose-bumps. She envisioned Madam Evensen, on her way to the early morning service on Christmas Day, but had gotten up too early and went to the church in the middle of the night on Christmas Eve. The streets had been quiet; Madam Evensen hadn't met even one person on the way. When she had entered the church she sat in her usual place in the front pew. She glanced around and thought the folks looked pale and peculiar, as if they were dead. Madam Evensen didn't see anyone she knew, but it seemed she had seen many of them before. No one was coughing or clearing their throats, like folks usually do in church. It was so quiet that she was horror-stricken. Then the woman next to her bent and whispered in her ear, "Put your coat back on and leave. If you wait they'll put an end to you. It's the dead who are holding Christmas service."

Was it true dead people could come back? Elise trembled and pulled the shawl tighter around her shoulders, looking nervously to both sides. The streets were still quiet. The gate to Albertsen, the wagon-driver, was open but no one was around. She heard his old horse neighing, whinnying and stomping his hooves in the tight stall. Maybe he was missing his daily tramping through the streets.

Maybe Pappa was sitting in Our Saviors Church with all the other ghosts right now? With his *skyggelua* pulled down over his forehead, a filthy vest missing every other button and patches on his pants. Nothing in the telling of the "Christmas Eve from Yesteryears" said the dead were dressed differently from when they'd been alive.

Or was he in heaven, just like the minister had said? Maybe God had forgiven him for all his sins because he had once been a decent man.

She tried to bring back a picture of him before he had started drinking. When he'd had a steady job at Seilduken and came home for lunch. He'd had a glint in his eyes, Pappa had. He told them tall tales from his sailor days that made them laugh out loud, and he played one-man theatre for them. It hurt to think that he'd been so good at playing the role of a drunken sailor.

She had a lump in her throat. She swallowed, blinked several times trying to hold back the tears. She gave up and let them run down her cheeks. She remembered Sunday trips down to the harbor, when Pappa stood and pointed to the freighter boats and told about the time he'd been caught in the middle of a hurricane in the Arabian Sea. He'd been a deckhand on a steamboat, named *Idefjord*. The waves had been as high and dark as the mountains surrounding them. And he told them about swaying palm trees and the hot, burning tropical sun. It sounded so real she almost felt the burning hot sun prickle her back. And he told them about the slum quarters on the outskirts of a city in Madagascar, the houses made from rusted tin cans that were so hot in the tropical sun that you could fry an egg on the roof. He told them, too, about babies lying and screaming in the midst of dust, sand and rubbish, and about old people who'd been laid out in the sand and burning-hot sun to die. Pappa had told the stories so well that she had seen it all in front of her, smelled the smells, heard the sounds and laughed and cried at the same time.

He should have never given up sailing, she thought for a moment. Then he wouldn't have sunk so low. It was the boring and tedious work at Seilduken that had ruined him. He wasn't made for standing still behind a machine in the same spot fourteen hours a day and afterwards going home to an exhausted, weary wife and a bunch of noisy kids. He had gypsy-blood running through his veins; he needed air under his wings and to wander around from place to place. If he had remained at sea he would have come up the ranks and become a ship's officer. He could have sent money home for the family and come home twice a year, good-natured and happy with bags full of gifts. Even if they would have missed him, it would have been so much better than seeing him come home depressed, downcast and drunk, night after night, until in the end he lost his job and resorted to hanging around on the streets for days on end.

It was their mother who had begged him to stay ashore. It hadn't been right, Elise thought now.

Her thoughts shifted to Johan. What would she say if he suddenly one day said that he'd signed onto a merchant marine ship, would sail away and wouldn't be back for half a year?

She had come as far as the place in Møllergate that gives out clothes to children of poor families. She remembered the shame she felt when Mamma had brought them here. When they came out with arms loaded down with used wooden-soled shoes and thick homespun woolen clothes wrapped in brown paper, they had bumped into two girls from her school class. Two who lived in three room apartments, their fathers were carpenters and their mothers didn't have to work but stayed home and took care of the family. They had looked her up and down, and gave her that "better than you" look that only young girls can do. When they had passed them, Elise heard them giggling and laughing about poor kids and whispering, "They wear *those* clothes." As if her family had chosen poverty and it was their own fault.

Not so far to go now. She had read somewhere that some people died with a blissful smile and peaceful look on their faces, but it was hard to imagine that Pappa had much to smile about when he had died fighting the icy river. There hadn't been much peace in his face either as he had stood in the middle of the kitchen last night, screaming obscenities at her, "To hell wid ya. I'm gonna teach ya, girl!" just before his fist came flying at her.

Tears pressed and ran down her cheeks; she wiped her eyes and nose on a corner of her *skaut* and talked hard to herself. What was the sense in crying over a father who'd done nothing but drink up all their money, make such a racket in the stairwell that Fru Evertsen and the tenement manager constantly came out and scolded at him, a father who swore and cursed, flicked their ears so hard that they rang, and beat their mother when he was at his worst. The sailor that had once stood at the harbor and told them about swaying palm trees and a tropical sun was long gone and would never return.

Finally she was there. Feeling a combination of shame and fear she mumbled who she was and why she was there, consoling herself that she had nothing to fear. No one but the street-girls knew that Johan had thrown Pappa out, and she was sure they wouldn't say anything, at least not to the police.

A doctor in a white coat came out from the room where she was told to go. Her hands were freezing and her body was shaking, even though the fast walking had made her warm.

A body laid on the table with a white sheet covering it. The constable pulled the sheet away from the face and looked at her. He wanted an answer.

She nodded and turned away. Tears came again, her whole body shaking as if with a very high fever. There was no doubt, it was her father, but it wasn't him. Stiff and yellow, his face all swollen and puffy. And so small. He who had once been the most handsome man in the world, her mother had said. There was neither a blissful smile nor a peaceful look on his face. He was just a dead body on a table --- an ashen face with closed eyes, hands folded stiffly and unnaturally on his chest. It was gruesome.

The constable helped her outside. "There, there," he said clumsily. "It'll be okay, Miss. Time heals all wounds."

What nonsense, Elise thought. As if time would erase all the painful images in her mind; her father screaming and shouting at her, with bloodshot eyes and drooling from a toothless mouth, or the image of his dead body lying on a naked table. They would always be there, forever and ever.

Thank God they hadn't mentioned a word about Johan, she comforted herself on the way home; after she'd signed some papers. She was sure the street-girls were sleeping it off in a dirty, dark room somewhere down at Vaterland. Maybe they would have forgotten all about it by tomorrow?

If she had only followed them down the steps, and not left it all to Johan.

Even though Johan had shouted to her to go in to Mamma, she shouldn't have listened to him. She could have followed them and made sure nothing out of the ordinary happened. She could have gotten a glimpse of Pappa when he staggered away and known for sure the fist-fights had nothing to do with the drowning. Now both she and Johan would agonize with doubt and wonder about what had actually happened.

When she came home the kitchen was full of folks. Hilda sat at the kitchen table, her face red and puffy from crying, with Fru Evertsen, Valborg's mother, Fru Thoresen and Fru Evertsen's sister around her. Two of them were sitting and two were standing. The coffee kettle was on the table, with some cups Elise didn't recognize, and a plate full of two-*øres* store-bought cakes. She was about to ask if they were having a coffee klatch, but managed to hold back.

Hilda stood up and looked at her, questioningly.

Elise nodded. "It was Pappa."

"How...? I mean..."

"He looked like he was sleeping. Now they'll transport him to Nordre Gravelund in the *likkjerra*. The minister will be here soon."

The other four women looked at her with mixture of greedy curiosity and overwhelming desire to be the first to know.

"Did ya hear if 'e fell in or..." Fru Evertsen stopped abruptly and looked with frustration at the others.

Elise shook her head. "No one knows, and I don't think we'll ever know, but I think he slid on the ice and fell. Drunk as he was," she added, fighting the tears.

They all nodded.

"How's Mamma doing?"

Hilda blew her nose and wiped her eyes, still sobbing and shook her head.

Elise walked over to the *kammers* door. "I don't think there should be so many here when the minister comes."

The women got the message, gathered their coffee cups, took the cake plate and got ready to leave. Hilda was going down with Fru Evertsen to borrow a black shawl.

Elise went into the *kammers*. She saw through the cheesecloth-thin curtains, a pale winter sun shining on the rooftops across the way.

Mamma lay with her eyes open, staring into the air. She turned her head slowly when she heard Elise come in.

Elise tried to force a smile. "It was Pappa."

"Have you seen Kristian?"

"Kristian?" Elise gave her a puzzled look. She had expected her mother wanted to hear more, to hear what had really happened, to hear how Pappa had looked, to hear what the constables meant, but, instead she was asking about Kristian.

Mamma nodded and closed her eyes. "He disappeared."

"I'm sure he ran out to get rid of some anger. He'll be back when he's hungry."

Mamma didn't answer. "Peder is downstairs with Johan," she said instead, opening her eyes.

"That's good for him. Peder looks up to Johan."

Her mother's eyes met hers. "You'll have to take care of Peder. You might not get anywhere with Kristian, but Peder..." She didn't say more, only a small sigh came through her dry lips.

"Don't worry, Mamma, we'll take care of Peder. And Kristian, too. Johan will talk to him, and I'm sure he'll be okay. But let's not talk about that now. First you must get well."

Mamma shook her head slowly. "Look truth in the eye, Elise, it'll make you strong. Courageous are those who dare to meet uncertainty with open eyes."

Elise looked at her with astonishment. There was no doubt Mamma must be feeling better. She had spoken more in the last few days than she had in the last several weeks. "I think God wants you to live, Mamma. At least now that Pappa is no longer with us."

Mamma closed her eyes without responding, but when Elise stood looking at her, she saw tears escaping from under her eyelashes. She turned and went quietly into the kitchen.

Just them Peder came in. He was holding a *ti-øres kremmerhus* of red sugar candy in his hand.

"Did you get that from Johan?" She asked.

Peder shook his head. "Two strangers gave it to me."

"Two strangers?" Elise asked wide-eyed.

"Two women-folk. Dey had red mout's and curly bangs. One of dem grinned da whole time."

Elise held her breath. "Where did you meet them?"

"Down in da street."

"I thought you were with Johan."

"I was der for a while, but den I'eard Evert hollerin' and run down to see whad it was. The two of dem stood der and wanted to find Johan. Dey gave me dis to go get 'im."

Elise could hardly breathe. "What did they look like?"

"I said dey had red mout's and curly bangs. One of dem was grinnin' all da time, even if dere wasn't nothin' to grin about."

"Oh, Lord!" Elise gasped under her breath. It had to be the two street-girls. The two that had seen the fist-fight last night.

Chapter 11

Her first impulse was to run down and ask Johan what that was about, but she heard footsteps in the stairwell and knew she had to wait.

The old minister came in, followed by Kristian. Elise looked from her brother to the minister and back to her brother again. Kristian glanced off in the other direction.

The minister took quick short breaths, groaning after climbing the steps and sank down on one of the kitchen stools, exhausted. "This is a sad state of affairs," he sighed. "Deep down he was a good man, your father. Deep down."

Elise glanced back at Kristian wondering where he had been and why he came home with the minister. Maybe the minister had seen the two street-girls down in the entryway, and maybe Kristian knew something about what had happened.

The minister started talking about the Lord, the Lord who gave, and the Lord who took away, and praised be the name of the Lord. Then he said a lot of things about death that Elise didn't understand, and she was too distracted to pay attention, anyway. She wanted desperately to go down to the second floor and ask Johan what the street-girls had wanted, but it didn't look like the minister would be leaving soon. His grey thinning hair was damp from the strenuous walk up the steps. He breathed heavily and coughed with a squeaky sound, which sounded like Mamma's cough.

Elise wondered if he was sick and decided she should pay better attention. Then he said something about "no sparrow falls to the ground unless it was God's will" and Elise thought that if God decided everything, why hadn't He gotten Pappa to stop drinking instead falling in the river, especially when He knew their mother was sick, Hilda was going to have a baby and Peder and Kristian needed a grownup to look after them for a few more years. But she became so preoccupied staring at the minister's double chins, jiggling up and down when he talked, that she forgot to pay attention. The only thing she heard was that the Poorhouse would pay for the funeral and he would be buried inside the fence far on the east side of the Nordre Gravelund.

Finally after the minister left, Elise was able to talk to Kristian. He and Peder had stood pressed against the wall when the minister was there, Kristian with his cap between his hands and a curious scowl on his face and Peder eagerly waiting to open his *ti-øres kremmerhus* of sugar candy. Although she had been upset that Kristian had run away, she softened when she saw how small and lost he looked today. "Where have you been?" she gently asked.

"Nowhere."

She stroked his hair. "That's how life is, Kristian. Some live a short life, some live a long life, but that's how it is with all of us."

"It don't bother *me* none. I never saw 'im anyway!" He clenched his lips tightly and blinked back the tears.

She went over to her secret hiding place and found the little yellow tin box that Pappa had used for storing his pipe tobacco. It had words from a foreign country printed on it: "Hills Badminton Smoking Mixture" and it held her entire fortune, ten *ti-ører* coins adding up to one *krone*. She had started saving last summer and so far had resisted the temptation to use any of it. Johan had told her not to touch her savings when she'd had to borrow from him that day to pay the rent. He was the only one who knew her secret. She quickly grabbed a *ti-øre* and handed it to Kristian before she might change her mind. "Go down to the store and buy a *kremmerhus* of sugar candy so you'll have one, too."

Kristian looked at her wide-eyed, and in a flash he was out the door with Peder on his heels.

Elise went into Mamma. "He's gone, Mamma. The minister. I wouldn't let him come in to you, since you said you didn't want to see him."

Her mother shook her head. "Why would he want to see *me*?"

Elise didn't say anything. Her mother had grown up at Ulefoss, where her father had been a worker at the foundry. She had always felt the church was there for the factory owner and his family, never for the workers.

"He sent his regards saying he'll come back when you're feeling better."

A thin, bitter smile slipped over Mamma's pale lips.

"I have to run down to ask Johan something," she continued. "I won't be long."

Mamma nodded and closed her eyes again.

Elise found Johan sitting alone in the kitchen, reading an old newspaper. "What has happened?" Elise gave him a frightened look. "I heard the street-girls were back and wanted to talk to you."

Johan put the newspaper down on the table and stood up. "Come in and have a *kaffesvett*, Elise. You could use it. Don't worry about the girls," he continued, taking a coffee cup from the rack. "I think they disappeared long before I threw your father out."

"But why did they come back now? What did they want?"

Johan shrugged his shoulders and seemed a bit embarrassed. "I think they came because they are that kind, you know."

Elise finally understood. "To seduce *you*, you mean?"
Johan nodded.

Elise stared at him. No, it really wasn't so strange, as handsome as Johan was, especially when thinking about the nasty, ugly, old men they'd gotten their hooks into last night. "So they didn't say anything about what happened?"

Johan shook his head.

"Had they heard anything? Did they know that Pappa..." Elise bit her lip and swallowed hard.

He shook his head again, came and wrapped his arms around her. "Elise, everything will be okay," he whispered in her ear. "When summer comes again and it's warm up in the meadow, we'll stroll up there on Saturday evenings and you will have forgotten all your problems."

She leaned into his broad chest, smelled the scent of coffee, tobacco, kerosene and his warm man's body, and already felt some of the pain beginning to disappear.

Later when she went up again, Hilda, Peder and Kristian were all in the kitchen. Kristian sat with his *kremmerhus* absorbed in crunching the sugar candy. Hilda sat crying, and Peder patted her arm clumsily trying to comfort her, "Now 'e is sittin' up in da clouds, Hilda, and 'e's looking down on us. Up dere, dere ain't no beer joints, ain't no moonshine, 'e's sober all da time."

Hilda cried even harder. Her emaciated body shook.

Elise brought out potatoes, ladled water into the tin basin and started peeling. Hilda had just brought up water from the town pump where the women often gathered and exchanged "the latest news." It was ice cold. Elise's hands were red and cracked from before, and now they ached when she put them in the freezing cold water.

It was Sunday, and she had sacrificed and bought *fleskebiter*. They all needed it today.

It seemed many days since Fru Evertsen had come and told them the shocking news. Her fear that it had been Hilda still held its grip. It was hard enough losing Pappa, but it would have been a thousand times worse if it had been Hilda.

All four ate together. At first nobody talked. Sadness hung over them. An unnatural strange mood. Like that day when Magda on the Corner's daughter got her hair caught in the machine at the mill. Everyone had screamed hysterically, but The Frog hadn't managed to stop the machine before her head... Elise forced the thought away.

"Whad do you t'ink happened to 'im, Elise?" Peder looked at her with huge, inquiring eyes.

"I think he slid on the ice and couldn't hold on."

"'Cause 'e was drunk?"

Elise nodded.

"Evert says he had been in a fist-fight." The words came from Kristian as casually as if he was telling them the gas lamp in the street had been smashed. He stuffed a big chunk of potato in his mouth and gazed off into space.

Elise's heart almost stopped beating.

Hilda turned abruptly to her brother. "You can't believe everything Evert says, he fantasizes more than Valborg."

Kristian scowled, "He saw 'im!"

"Oh really, Evert was out that late at night?" Hilda's voice was sarcastic. "I'm sure Hermansen let him do that."

Kristian bit his lip hard and dropped the conversation.

Elise feverishly cut into her *fleskbiter* trying not to look at any of them. Could Evert really have been out in the middle of the night and had seen what had happened? Had he seen Johan throw Pappa out head first? Maybe he'd even seen him bleeding, so dizzy and out of it from the fall that he didn't know where he was going and stumbled right into the river.

Her head was cold, and her ears were ringing. Evert gossiped as much as Valborg, or maybe more. If he had seen Johan during the scuffle it wouldn't be long before everybody in the whole street knew about it. Then someone with an axe to grind could go straight to the police station in Møllergate 19.

She knew many held a grudge against them, a carry-over from when all four had jobs – Mamma, Pappa, Hilda and herself. Those who hadn't found work thought it unfair that four from the Løvlien family had jobs. Some even whispered about "brown nosing with the director" and some taunted them openly, and had come with flippant remarks like "dey t'ink dey're better 'an us" and "dey try to talk like folks on da west-side."

It's dangerous to be different, she thought with a heavy sigh. Ever since Mamma had come from Ulefoss to look for work in Kristiania she had tried to talk like she thought everyone did in the capital city. She hadn't noticed that the most of the workers along Akerselva didn't come from Kristiania at all, but from the countryside and had made up their own language.

Strangely enough Johan was different. Both he and his sister, Anna, did not speak like their mother, but they were still respected.

What would happen to Johan if the constables at Møllergate 19 became suspicious that he and Pappa had been in a brawl just before he fell in the river? Her hand on her mouth, she froze, trembling with fear.

"Whad's wrong with ya, Elise?" Peder looked at her with fright in his eyes.

"I'm so freezing cold!"

"As hot as it is in 'ere no'?"

"It's because of Pappa," Hilda jumped in. "When something sad happens, we get cold. I've been cold ever since…" She bit her lip and stopped.

Elise knew what she was about to say, "ever since I came home this morning."

"Pappa must 'a froze a lot," Peder said with a shiver. "Imagin', fallin' into dat icy slush."

"Shush!" Stop talking about it." Hilda hit the knife on the table so hard that it vibrated and "sang."

Suddenly Kristian stood up so abruptly that his stool almost tipped over. He grabbed his *skyggelua* from the nail on the wall and stormed out the door.

"See," Hilda sputtered. "He ran out 'cause of what you said."

"I was only sayin' 'ow it is," Peder said apologetically, with downcast eyes.

Elise tried to pull herself together. She had to be both mother and father now. Well, she had been both for most of the past year, but now it was for real. "Now, now," she quieted him. "Peder, it's like you said, but Kristian hurts, too, you know, even if he's not showing it."

Peder looked at her with huge, innocent eyes. "Does 'e 'urt, too"?

Elise nodded. "He's not like you. Instead of crying, he slams doors and runs away or looks mad."

There was stillness around the table.

"What did Mamma say?" Hilda asked, sobbing.

Elise shook her head. "She doesn't say much. Maybe she's been expecting it would happen sometime."

"She's not cryin'?" Peder looked alarmed.

"Of course, she's sad and crying." Hilda gave him an irritated look. "But not everybody cries as loud as you do."

"Shhhh, Hilda. You're forgetting that Peder is only eight years old. When you were eight years old, you screeched if somebody just teased you a little."

Hilda sent her an indignant glance and got up from the table. "I'm going out for a walk!"

Elise followed with her eyes, but didn't say a word. If Hilda found comfort elsewhere, she was allowed that on a day like today.

"Go into Mamma with some food, Peder," she said instead. "When she sees that it's you, maybe she'll eat a little bit."

Peder didn't have to be asked twice. Meanwhile Elise started clearing the table. Evert filled her thoughts! It was urgent that she talk with him and find out what he had seen...

Chapter 12

The diffuse darkness of Norway's short winter days had set in. The gas lamps were mystically wrapped with dimly flickering rings against a dark night sky. A horse and sleigh with ringing bells came and stopped in front of Sagene Folkebad, which had been established May 10, 1900, with money donated from *Christiania Brændevinssamlag*. That was written above the door, in any case. The building was so grand and beautiful that a few years ago Elise had daydreamed that she was the daughter of a wealthy man and lived in a house just like it.

A hunch-backed old man walked towards her; otherwise it was quiet in the street. The snow kept falling, and the tracks from the sleigh would soon be covered. From an open window she could smell fried *fleskebiter*, a sign that it wasn't only she who'd indulged and used money for an extra good Sunday dinner. The only sound was a dog barking in the distance.

She wondered if the rumors were true, that Hermansen - the Poorhouse had placed Evert in his care and gave him money - was a man you should stay as far away from as possible.

She shuddered, gritted her teeth and walked faster. It was necessary to talk to Evert before he started spreading tall-tale rumors about what he'd seen.

Soon she was in Østgaardsgate and looked for the right number.

The entrance was pitch-dark. The stairwell smelled of ammonia, but the strong stench from the outhouse overpowered all. She had to hold her breath until she got past.

Her heart was beating hard when she knocked on Hermansen's door.

It was quiet inside, maybe no one was home. Her first thought was relief. She could turn and run back home, but she knew it would just be delaying the matter. She knocked on the door one more time, and not long after, she heard stumping steps trudging closer.

The door opened a crack, and Hermansen peered at her, a kerosene lantern in his hand.

"May I please speak with Evert?"

Wha's wrong?"

"Nothing. I'm just bringing him a message from my little brother."

"Hmmm." Hermansen looked at her with skepticism. Then he turned slowly and shuffled through a door. Soon after Evert came out.

"Whad'aja want?" His voice was cranky and he looked suspicious of her.

"Kristian told me you saw Pappa last night," she whispered, in case Evert had been out late without permission and Hermansen stood listening behind the door.

He didn't answer.

"Is it true?"

"Ya think I'm lyin'?"

"I just thought it was strange that you were out so late."

He shrugged his shoulders. "I din't know what time it was."

Elise put her hand in her apron pocket and pulled out a *ti-øre* coin. Now there are two gone from Pappa's tobacco tin, she thought wistfully. "I'll give you this if you tell me the truth and promise not to talk to anybody else."

Evert stared hungrily at the shiny *ti-øre*. "I saw him come flyin' out the door, and he fell head first on the sidewalk.

Afterwards he got up on his feet and stumbled towards the river."

"Did you see anybody else? Why did he fall down?"

Evert shook his head. "He'd been drinkin'. The other one, too."

Elise nodded. "Ja, that's why he slid on the ice." She pressed the *ti-øre* coin into his hand and turned around to leave.

"But, that ain't why 'e drowned," Evert shouted behind her.

Abruptly she turned towards him. "What do you mean?"

At that very moment, Hermansen came up behind Evert. "Whad's goin' on here?!" Both suspicion and irritation thundered in his voice.

Evert shrunk together before her eyes. "Nothin', Hermansen. Just Peder's sister wanted to know where 'e is, but I ain't seen 'im."

"Don't jus' stand der in the door lettin' cold air come in!"

Evert turned and slammed the door right in her face.

Elise stood for a moment in deep thought before she turned around and started to go home. "What in the world had Evert meant?"

They went to bed early that night. Long after the lamp had been blown out, Elise heard sniffles from her brothers' bed, irritated grunts from Kristian and new sniffles from Peder again.

"Be quiet! Shut up!" Hilda called out, irritated. "I need to get up at five, let me sleep."

It wasn't strange that *she* was tired when she'd been gone all last night, Elise thought and wondered where she could have been all those hours?

She heard Mamma cough, a dry, whistling sound that cut right through her. She remembered what Fru Evertsen had said, "Be glad as long as she's not coughin' up blood." She hadn't seen any yet, and she checked every day. "Dear God," she prayed silently, "please don't let it happen with Mamma like it did with Pappa. How could I possibly marry Johan then, and how will the boys manage without parents?" She felt the lump in her throat again.

Hilda had enough as it was, and the *verksmester*, Herr Paulsen, had promised "to take care of it." Maybe he would find Hilda a house-maid job with someone he knew? Then he would be able to see his son or daughter without anyone in the house knowing the child was his. That's what he's planning. He would no doubt convince Hilda to lie about who the father was. Maybe he would tell a tear jerking story to his friends about the poor fatherless baby and the orphaned factory girl who'd lost her father in a tragic drowning accident and her mother had tuberculosis. Maybe he would use that to convince them to take Hilda into their home. Then Hilda would be a housemaid in a home filled with plush furniture, electric lights, thick carpets on the floor and lovely paintings in heavy, gilded frames hanging on the walls, and Elise would be sitting at home alone with Peder and Kristian. And Johan would lose his patience after a while and find himself another girl. As handsome and good looking as he was, even the street-girls from Vaterland had come all the way to Sagene to see him.

She tossed and turned on the straw mattress until a heavy sleep with bad dreams slowly came over her.

She awakened wet with sweat, even though it was freezing cold in the *kammers*.

She had dreamt she was standing up in the front of an electric streetcar beside the driver. Johan was there, too. He had been angry, shouting at the driver who in turn became angry and drove faster and faster. Suddenly there opened in front of them a beautiful, rolling landscape filled with lush green trees and colorful flowers. When she saw its splendor, she forgot Johan and the streetcar driver, turned and ran to the back of the streetcar crying out over her shoulder, "I must get Pappa. I want to show him how beautiful it is here."

That wasn't a bad dream, she thought, amazed. With the exception of the two men arguing in the front of the streetcar, everything had been pleasant and good, almost supernaturally beautiful. Maybe it was heaven she had seen in front of the streetcar? The heaven Pappa had gone to? She hoped so.

Half asleep, she pulled herself up from the straw mattress. A new day was ahead of her, a long, tedious day at the factory. She fumbled her way to the kitchen, frozen and barefoot, struck a match and lit the kerosene lamp. Shivering, she poured cold water into the wash basin and quickly washed before putting on her undershirt, underpants, and black scratchy stockings. Her thoughts returned to Evert. Did he know more, or did he only want to make it more interesting? Maybe he wanted another *ti-øre*?

The *kammers* door opened slowly and Hilda came in, yawning. She shivered and wrapped her arms around her body. "Why's it so cold in here? Why haven't you started the fire?"

Elise scowled. "Why haven't *you* started the fire?" She opened the woodstove oven door, took out a couple pieces of wood she'd put there to dry out enough to burn. She put them with kindling into the burning chamber of the woodstove and lit the fire. Then she dressed quickly.

"It must be even colder outside," Hilda moaned. "I just don't know how I'll handle it. There are holes in the soles of both of my boots, the snow gets in and quick-as-a-wink my feet are soaking wet."

"Then you'll have to go see the shoemaker."

"And where will I get money for that? And what should I wear in the meantime?"

Elise thought for a moment.

"Maybe the Salvation Army can help you. I was thinking of going there tonight."

Hilda looked at her, puzzled, but Elise didn't want to explain. She had not been in the Temple for a long time. It must seem strange that she was going only one day after the accident.

She was still tired when she left for work; she had taken care of Mamma and gotten Peder and Kristian up and gave them breakfast. She had also washed the dishes, washed two pair of boys' stinky darned-socks and hung them up to dry over the woodstove, as well as stoking the fire in the *kammers*. Hilda was supposed to help with the morning chores, but suddenly she was nauseated and ran down to the backyard to throw up.

Elise was so exhausted she could have laid down right there on the steps and laid there the whole day, even though she hadn't done more this morning than usual.

She felt miserable. She didn't even want to see Johan and hurried past his door, hoping to get to work unseen, but as soon as she came out to the sidewalk she heard quick steps behind her.

"Elise?"

She stopped and turned around. The gas lamp hadn't been fixed so it was dark. It was before six o'clock and the factory sirens hadn't yet begun to howl.

Johan came toward her. He seemed even larger in the early morning dawn.

"Is it you already?"

He laughed. "Don't I always leave at this time? You hurried by so fast I wondered if something is wrong. I mean..." He stopped and heard how stupid it sounded. Of course something was wrong.

"I feel miserable. I'd hoped I wouldn't meet anybody on my way out." Elise looked down.

He came over to her and pulled her close. "My sweet, silly girl. Don't you think I'd rather see you tired and sad than not see you at all?"

She smiled at him. He smelled of tobacco and smoke from the stove, she drew in a deep breath and closed her eyes. "Johan, I'm so happy I have you in my life."

He stroked the *skaut* on her head with his masculine hand. "And you think I don't want to see you, the most beautiful girl in all of Sagene?"

She could only laugh. It was wonderful to hear, even if she knew it wasn't true. Then she became serious again. "I went to see Evert yesterday. Kristian told me Evert saw the fist-fight."

She noticed Johan's body stiffen. "Evert? Was he out that late?"

"He said he was. I gave him *ti-øre* to keep quiet."

"And what did he see?" Johan stood still, but she could tell he was nervous, probably scared that he had hit Pappa too hard.

"He said he saw Pappa flying out the door, and fell head first on the sidewalk. Afterwards he got up and staggered down towards the river."

Johan didn't say anything. He seemed to expect more.

"Just as I was leaving, Evert shouted something more. He said that wasn't the reason that Pappa drowned."

Johan still didn't say anything.

"Evert does say so many strange things," she added, mostly to calm her own thoughts. She didn't want to worry him either, and it was true that Evert told many lies and gossiped.

"I was thinking of going down to the Temple tonight. I thought maybe…" she stopped, searching for the words. "I have so many peculiar thoughts going through my head right now. Maybe it would help to hear some uplifting words. And they sing so beautifully."

She smiled. She really had no right to look forward to songs and music, not when her father was laying in the cooler in Storgata 40 and would soon be buried at Nordre Gravlund.

"I'll come with you then." His voice was calm now.

The factory sirens started howling, first one, then the next one and the next. The sound cut through to the bone and marrow as always, but today the sound was extra irritating.

She pulled away. "I've got to run." She turned toward the gate. "I wonder where Hilda is."

"I've got to run, me too! See you tonight, Elise." Then he ran off.

Elise stood for a moment, but didn't dare wait longer so started on her way.

Everything was frozen, the slush had turned to ice and the tracks from the horse-drawn wagons were hard, filled with thick patches of ice. The cold bit her face, and it wasn't long before both her fingers and toes were numb. Her thoughts returned to Hilda, who was already freezing before she went out and had holes in the soles of both boots.

Someone was standing by the bridge exactly at the spot where Pappa had been pulled up on the bank. When she got closer she could see some of the girls from Hjula. As soon as they saw it was her under the gas lamp, they stuck their heads together. The roaring waterfalls made it impossible to catch what they were saying, but from their scowling glances she understood. They'll be busy now, those gossip-spreaders, she thought with indignation. It wasn't hard to imagine what they were talking about. Had Pappa drowned himself intentionally, had he slid on the ice or had someone pushed him?

She hurried past without looking at them and dreading the day at the mill. She was sure it would be the same there: Whispering, gossiping and peculiar glances.

She had just come in the door when she ran into the night-guard. He looked away, embarrassed. "My condolences," he mumbled without looking at her.

She nodded, not knowing how to answer; she didn't really know what that meant. Should she say "thank you?"

Nearly everyone was there now. When she came into the hall, everyone turned their attention to her. No one said a word. She noticed two girls walked over to Valborg and whispered something to her, and Valborg whispered back. I'm sure she thinks she knows more than anyone else, Elise thought and tried not to care about all the curious glances. For the very first time she impatiently waited for the machines to start up.

All of a sudden her eyes opened wide. Hilda came in, with the *verksmester*.

It became deathly silent. Herr Paulsen stood for everyone to see. He cleared his throat. "I'm sure everyone has heard of the tragedy that's happened. Elise and Hilda's father fell in the falls last night and drowned. It was awfully icy and snowing hard. He more than likely didn't see how close he was to the edge of the river, slid and fell in. That's also what the police think."

Elise noticed some of the girls steal glances at each other, grimacing. She knew what they were thinking. It wasn't strange that a drunkard hadn't seen where he was going.

"I ask all of you to be extra helpful to Hilda and her sister today, and in the days ahead, especially you who have Hilda as a bobbin girl. Those of you who have lost a good father or mother can surely understand what she's going through."

There he forgot himself, Elise thought, he's talking like it only concerns Hilda.

The girls exchanged glances, again, surprised that the *verksmester* spoke so warmly about Hilda. Now the gossip would really start to fly, Elise thought. If none of them had been envious of them before, now they would be!

The *verksmester* turned and gave Hilda a fatherly pat on her shoulder before going towards the door. Both the spinners and the bobbin girls followed Hilda curiously with their eyes as she walked to her work place. They have apparently lost interest in *me*, Elise thought, feeling relieved. As long as they didn't add two and two together once they discovered Hilda was pregnant.

She had never thought a day could be so long as today. Her back ached, her toes were frozen and her fingers were hurting and stiff.

Finally, lunch time. She searched to the other end of the hall for Hilda to walk home with her, but saw the girls flocking around her. More and more came. Hilda barely managed to signal Elise to go on home without her. Were they bothering her or were they just curious?

Elise left the hall wondering. The girls were obviously not shunning Hilda; quite the opposite, they were fighting to get closer to her. Was it because the *verksmester* had been so fatherly towards her? She shook her head, not understanding.

It wasn't unthinkable. It could be beneficial to be close to the *verksmester's* favorite.

She ran most of the way home, not just because she was cold, but she was worried about Mamma. One never knew how a seriously ill person would react to the news of death. In spite of all the hurt and pain they had lived through because of Pappa's drunkenness the last two years, Mamma had never said a bad word about him. Elise didn't understand. If it had been her, she would have pounded on the table, chewed him out and refused to let him come home if he couldn't sober up. But, Mamma had always defended him; talked about how kind he had been before the "poison got hold of him," how handsome and charming he had been when he was younger and how good he was at singing and dancing.

"You inherited your beautiful singing voice from him, Elise," she used to say. A beautiful voice hadn't helped one bit when he got drunk, swore and hit them, she thought, a bitter taste in her mouth.

A wonderful, golden glow in the winter sky was mirrored in the glossy river water that hadn't frozen yet. It is like an omen from above, she thought and hurried home. Anxiety knotted her stomach. Kristian and Peder had gone to school several hours ago and Mamma lay alone as always. Johan was at Seilduken, his mother was at the factory, and Anna lay alone in bed, just like Mamma. So helpless...With no one to call to if something happened, no one to talk to if they were afraid.

If only one of the slum sisters would come by, but they had so many others to take care of, others who had it much worse than them. Especially down at Vaterland, where the street-girls and "outcasts" hung out and there were tramps living in every other entryway and moonshine sold in every other shop. In addition, the Salvation Army needed workers to take care of all the children at The Crib at Sagene and in Bakkegata. She had heard that in the course of one year, many thousands of infants were left there when their mothers were at work. What would the mothers do without the folks in the Salvation Army?

When she comes to the Temple tonight, she'll try to talk with one someone. Tell them what had happened with their father and how sick their mother was. Maybe they had a solution.

Once she had met Othilie Tonning, the General for the slum sisters. She was a remarkable woman. Johan had told Elise that before Othilie had converted she had been actively involved in the women's voting rights movement. She had a short haircut, like a boy, and smoked cigars. It was said she became enthusiastic for the Salvation Army because they gave the same rights and possibilities to women as the men had. Now she was dedicating her whole life to helping needy folks. She had also started hanging up Christmas kettles, so the money collected in them could give the destitute a better Christmas. With this money they bought clothes and shoes for the needy. Johan had said, too, that Evert had received food and clothes from them. Maybe they could help Hilda with a pair of boots, without holes in the soles?

"Think about miracles and they happen," she said to herself when she saw one of the Salvation Army sled drivers coming from their woodshed in Urtegate with a sled full of firewood. The sled was slinging from side to side on the rough, partly frozen ice tracks. The old, tired horse panted so hard that his breath hung over him like a cloud. The sled driver was frozen stiff, his hands red and cracked, his eyes watered and icicles stuck in his beard. He was one of the lucky ones who had gotten a bed at the Herberget in Urtegate. Elise had heard they had 130 beds, and the men got cheap food from the soup kitchens and a roof over their head by working in the wood shed, chopping and delivering wood.

Pappa could have certainly gotten a bed there, too. The thought came to her abruptly. Those who asked the Salvation Army soldiers for help almost always got it. But, Pappa would rather be a free man, drink and hang with street-girls than chop wood… She breathed a deep sigh.

"Do you have a few pieces of wood for me, too?" she shouted to the driver as he came nearer.

She had seen him before. He normally took the route between Sandakerveien, Østgaardsgate and Seilduksgata. He had an angry and guilty look, but when she took the time to stop and exchange a few friendly words, he thawed out and was almost friendly.

"You've got a job, you can take care of yourself," he grumbled.

"Pappa died yesterday and Mamma's bedridden. I also have my two younger brothers to support.

He stopped the old horse and studied her face with his squinty, watery look. "That wasn't your father who fell in the river?"

Elise nodded and looked down. She regretted saying it. Felt ashamed. It didn't feel right to stand here and talk about Pappa.

"Grab a sack, but hurry up, I'm freezing."

She didn't have to be told twice, grabbed one of the big sacks of chopped wood, shouted *tusen takk* and went off home with the valuable sack.

She tugged and pulled to get the heavy sack up the steps, but her thankfulness over the gift outweighed the strain. Happily she hurried into the kitchen, dropped the sack on the floor with a thud, brushed the small bits of wood off her clothes and walked quietly into the *kammers*.

To her surprise, Mamma was sitting up in bed. She sat with the Bible in her lap, folded hands and a joyful expression in her clear, blue eyes. Elise stood still for a moment, letting the wonderful sight sink in. It was as if something exalting, something holy, had come over Mamma.

"Are you feeling better, Mamma?" Elise's voice was cheerful.

Her mother's smile was weak. "I think so. I was able to read a little in the Bible."

"I've thought about going down to the Temple tonight, if you don't have anything against it."

Mamma looked up. "Why would I object? Those folks are inspired by God's spirit, Elise. They call themselves the "Hallelujah Army" and give hope to all who've lost faith that there is some good in this world."

Elise nodded eagerly. "I heard a funny story last time I was there," she started, encouraged by seeing Mamma looking so much better. "A woman was talking to one of the Salvation Army officers. The only thing she didn't like about them was the noisy drums. 'Do you like the church bells better?' he'd asked her. 'Yes, when the church bells ring, it's like they are calling, 'Come in! Come in!' said the woman. Then the Salvation Army officer replied, 'but, when you hear our drums beating, they're calling, 'Gather them in! Gather them in'!"

Her mother nodded seriously. "It's almost only well-dressed rich folks in church, but poor folks go to the Temple. That's the difference."

Elise looked at her. She remembered Mamma's bitterness and anger towards the church and the ministers at Ulefoss. "Will you eat some food, Mamma?"

"*Ja, takk,* if you'll cook oatmeal, I'd like a little."

"Is Johan going with you tonight?" Mamma asked abruptly, anxiety in her voice.

"Ja, I think so."

"I'd rather you didn't go without him, Elise."

Elise turned, surprised. "Why is that?"

Mamma looked worried. I am suddenly so worried. This with Pappa..." Her eyes filled with tears.

"But, you know why... I mean..."

Mamma nodded. "I know he was drunk, Elise. But, I don't think that's why he fell into the falls. He's been drunk so many times before without rambling into the river. Why should it happen now? When a person lays here like me, you have lots of time to think."

Elise looked questioningly at her.

"Don't ask me what I think, because I don't know, I just can't explain it. I only have this strange feeling that it was something else."

"Have you dreamed?" Elise looked at her as a cold shiver ran through. Mamma's dreams had come true several times. Almost every time it was about something unpleasant that would happen in the future.

Mamma didn't answer, but looked at her with concern. "I need you, Elise. We all do. Nothing can happen to you."

"Don't be afraid, as long as I have Johan, nothing can happen to me."

Her mother shook her head. "You're right, as long as you have Johan, you'll be safe."

But when Elise left to go back to the mill, she met Johan on the steps. He had been home for lunch, too. "I can't come with you to the Temple after all. I had forgotten there is a meeting at the Laborers Union tonight."

Elise gave him a frightened look, Mamma's words still ringing in her ears. Annoyed, she pushed it away. No one could dream what would happen; it was just coincidence when it did.

But she could not get rid of the uneasiness. It followed her the rest of day. She considered staying home, but Hilda needed new boots, and Mamma needed someone to come and look in on her. She couldn't be frightened by superstition.

After she'd made sure Peder and Kristian had done their school lessons and she'd given them something to eat, she hurried off without telling Mamma that Johan would not be going with her. She hadn't seen anything of Hilda.

Chapter 13

The weather had shifted during the day. It was wet and slushy and the fog hung heavy over the streets. The smell of fried herring escaped through open kitchen windows. People had finally come home from work and were staying inside.

The streets were deserted. Sleigh bells on a horse and sled jingled just around the corner, and on the other side some youngsters laughed and were making noise, but the roaring waterfalls were stronger than ever and overpowered most sounds.

After crossing over the bridge - without looking towards the spot where Pappa had been found - she chose to walk on Sagveien down to Maridalsveien, then up Akersbakken and past Gamle Aker Kirke. The Temple was in Pilestredet 22, which was a long walk.

It was strangely quiet everywhere this evening, she thought. Hardly anyone around. It seemed as if the city was bewitched. Where were all the people? As crowded as most folks lived, usually in any case, the kids were out in the evening, to get a little elbow room.

She had come to the top of the hill. She looked at the luxurious houses on the other side of the street. But, not crowded there, she thought. Many of the windows were lit up. Up there they had plenty of room...

Below her to the left was Our Saviors Cemetery, which seemed huge, dark and grim. The street lamps in Ullevaalsveien made the huge tree tops look like enormous, scary monsters.

What was it Mamma had dreamed? And what had she meant that Pappa hadn't fallen in the falls because he was drunk? A chill ran through her. The only thing she could think of was Johan had been a little rough with Pappa, and that had made him dizzy and he'd lost his balance.

It sounded like someone was coming up behind her, and she turned around quickly. It was a long way to the next street lamp, and the fog was heavy. She saw no one, the sound had stopped, and she didn't hear anything else.

She stood still holding her breath and listened. In the far distance she heard an automobile, and she imagined she could hear the clanging sound of a streetcar. A door slammed, a horse neighed in a backyard. Otherwise there was no sign of life.

Her uneasiness heightened. The thoughts of Madam Evertsen in Our Saviors Church came back. If it was true that the dead held midnight service in the church on Christmas Eve, maybe they could appear at other times and other places. Maybe Pappa blamed her that he had fallen in the river? If she hadn't chased him out the door, he would still be alive today. Agnes had told her the dead could seek revenge.

She hurried along. It helped a little to come down to Ullevaalsveien, with better street lamps, but as soon as she crossed over to Stensberggate, it was just as dark again. She walked still faster, half-running. She didn't dare look back, didn't look to her left or her right. There probably weren't as many drunks here as along Akerselva, but you could never be sure. And it wasn't the drunks that scared her. No, it was something else, something much more eerie, more dangerous. Madam Evertsen's words echoed in her ears. "Put your coat back on and leave. If you stay until the end they'll put an end to you..."

Could this be what Mamma had meant? Was she afraid Pappa would come back and seek revenge because he didn't get to live with them? Mamma had certainly heard every word, the walls were paper thin. Mamma knew what had happened, had lain trembling in her bed and heard Pappa cursing and swearing when Elise stood her ground, she'd heard the ear deafening slam when Johan came storming in. It must have been awful for her to understand that they fought, as helpless as she was. When she was told that he'd died, she'd no doubt had her own thoughts. But, she hadn't said anything. Not one word.

Finally she was close to Pilestredet. The thought of coming into the warm, brightly lit meeting hall gave her renewed strength. The walk had been a strain after the long day at the spinning mill, and it had been a long time since she'd had enough to eat.

She snuck in and sat on the back bench. In front of her sat row after row of hunched backs – darkly clad figures, just as hungry and emaciated as she was. Dead-tired after twelve to fourteen hour workdays, frozen both in body and soul, but still feeling a little spark of hope, or they wouldn't be here.

Way up at the front she saw cheerful and friendly people in blue uniforms. A young girl sat by the piano, and behind her sat other women with guitars ready to play.

The meeting started. Even as tired and exhausted as she was, and the warmth in the room made her body relax and sink together, she followed intently with what was being said. In the officer's speech, he referred to William Booth, the English man who had founded the Salvation Army: "While women weep, as they do now, I'll fight; while little children go hungry, as they do now, I'll fight; while men go to prison, in and out, in and out, as they do now, I'll fight; while there is a drunkard left, while there is a poor lost girl out on the streets, while there remains one dark soul without the light of God, I'll fight--I'll fight to the very end!"

Then he spoke about the good results the Salvation Army had achieved in England. Thousands of people who'd lived in sin, had begun to lead moral lives, drunkards had become teetotalers, criminals of the worst kind were leading blameless lives, theatres and dance halls of the worst sort had been converted to houses of God, and the taverns were emptier and emptier, as well as the prisons.

Was it really true that many drunkards had become teetotalers? Maybe Pappa could have been if I had convinced him to come here, Elise thought and a lump grew in her throat. She had never tried, hadn't thought there was hope for him. In any case, not the last year.

After the officer's speech, all folded their hands and prayed, and the band started to lead the hymn singing with drums, violins, trumpets and accordions. The music was lively and captivating, so different from in church, it almost made a person want to dance, she thought and straightened her back.

She sat there until the meeting was done, even though she noticed one person after another had slunk out before it was over. The Salvation Army soldiers left their seats and moved among those still sitting there. Elise thought about all the times she had been here, hoping no one would come and talk to her. She hadn't known what to say, afraid she would make promises she couldn't keep.

But today she wanted one of them to come to her.

She followed them in anticipation with her eyes, afraid they wouldn't have the time. So many wanted comforting words today.

A man glanced her way and moved in her direction, a young and handsome Salvation Army soldier, with a comforting smile. She could see that.

He sat down beside her. She was sitting alone in her row. "Is there something I can help you with?" He asked, looking at her.

She nodded and bowed her head in humiliation, regretting already that she'd hoped someone would come to talk to her.

"Just relax, I've got time," he continued. His voice was deep and reassuring. "Is there something you don't understand? Is there something we can pray about together?"

Elise shook her head. "I need a pair of boots, with no holes in the soles," she heard herself saying, and felt her face turn bright red. "It's not for me. It's for my sister."

He nodded and didn't seem upset by her bold request. "Of course, we can do that. We recently got in both boots and shoes from kind contributors. Is there something else you are wondering about?"

"Yes, I was wondering if one of the slum sisters could drop by and see Mamma. She lays alone almost the whole day."

"Is she sick?"

Elise nodded. "She has tuberculosis and has been bedridden since summer."

He looked at her with glowing warmth in his eyes. "Then it's not easy for you. Is there something else you'd like to talk about with me?"

Elise hesitated. Could she tell him the rest? She fidgeted.

"It'll be between you and me," he said calmly. "You don't have to worry that I'll tell anyone else."

"My father died yesterday," she whispered.

He didn't say anything, quietly waiting for her to continue.

"He was drunk and was found dead in the river."

The corners of his mouth twitched a little.

She drew in a deep breath, hesitating to continue, but decided not to hold anything back. "I chased him out." Elise bit her lip and fought the tears. "There were four of them.

Another drunkard and two street-girls. I didn't want Mamma to lay there and hear them so I ordered him to get out. He hit me, but I didn't give in to him. Then Johan came. There was a fist-fight and Pappa was thrown out into the street."

She quickly put her hand over her mouth. "Then I don't know what happened until he was found the next morning." Her voice tearful, she felt her chin quivering.

He put his hand gently over hers; it was warm, clean, with long fingers and short clipped nails. "And now you are wondering if the fist-fight had anything to do with his death?"

Elise nodded.

"You did the right thing throwing him out. It must have been unbearable for your mother listening to it, especially since he hit you. Tuberculosis is a serious illness."

Elise lowered her head and covered her eyes. "It's so terrible to think he was laying in the icy-slush... And I don't know if Johan hit him too hard."

"What does Johan say about it? Is he a neighbor?"

Elise nodded. "He lives one floor below us."

"And he heard the ruckus?"

Elise felt her face redden. "We're engaged. I think he was scared for me so he came up. This wasn't the first time it happened, but he'd never thrown Pappa out before."

"Be happy you have someone to look out for you. You need that. Let's fold our hands and pray together, pray that God will forgive both your father and your fiancé."

"And me," she added quickly.

He got up when the prayer was over. "Wait here a little. I'm going to find out if one of the slum sisters can visit your mother."

Elise looked at him and gathered her courage. "Can you also ask if they have warm boots?"

He smiled. "I haven't forgotten."

He came back with a middle aged woman. She had a pale, smiling face, and gray hair tucked in a tight bun under her uniform hat. Imagine looking so happy with so much poverty and sadness around her, Elise thought. The woman greeted her with a friendly hello, asked Elise her name, where they lived and promised to stop by in a few days.

The hall was nearly empty when Elise moved toward the door. As she was leaving, she heard a man's voice behind her. "I live in Akersbakken. We can walk together, if you want."

It was him, the young Salvation Army soldier. Elise turned around, smiling; she had dreaded walking home alone. "Thank you, I'd like that."

In the beginning they walked without saying a word. It was a little embarrassing walking with a strange man, but it helped that he was in his uniform, and everyone could see he was a Salvation Army soldier. And since he was only going as far as Akersbakken, she didn't have to walk beside him when she came to the bridge.

"Do you work in one of the factories?" He turned and glanced at her in the dimness of a street lamp.

She nodded. "At Nedre Vøien Spinning Mill."

"Are there many in your family?"

She shook her head. "It's only six of us. Five," she corrected herself quickly. "Kristian and Peder, who are my two younger brothers, Hilda, who is my sister, Mamma and me."

"Are you the only one working?"

"No, Hilda works, too. Kristian and Peder are only nine and eight years old and go to school."

"Do you live with another family?"

"No, we are lucky to have our kitchen for ourselves."

"So, when Hilda and you go to work at six o'clock in the morning, your sick mother is alone with the boys, and when they go to school there is no one else there?"

"Yes, but I come home during my lunch break."

"And when your brothers come back from school, they start a fire in the woodstove maybe?"

"Sometimes." Elise looked down. "It all depends on how much coal and firewood we have." Then she lifted her head and her voice got lighter. "Yesterday I got a full sack of wood for free from one of the Salvation Army firewood drivers."

"That's good to hear." He smiled at her.

Imagine that such a young man was spending his life helping others, she thought. She was sure he could have been a doctor, a minister or a director if he wanted. Instead he chose to work among the poor and sick - and for a pittance.

"The city is really quiet tonight," he commented, somewhat astonished.

She turned quickly towards him. "Yes, and that's why I'm glad to walk together. When I left home I had the feeling someone was following me." She half-heartedly laughed, immediately feeling embarrassed. "I don't like walking past the graveyard. It makes me think of Madam Evensen who saw all the ghosts in Our Saviors Church."

He laughed. "That's just a folktale."

"That might be true, but Agnes told me the dead can seek revenge."

"That's just more old folklore." His voice was serious now. "That's what they believed a long, long time ago, when folks thought that *åsgårdsreia* - the dead - came flying through the air on horses just before Christmas, and took with them those who hadn't behaved like they should. Or others who were outside at that moment."

Elise listened to him in astonishment. She didn't know about this. It was obvious he had lots of knowledge. A sudden thought struck her. Should she tell him about the brooch? Ask him what he thought she should have done and if she should have kept it? He had said all that she told him would be between them, that he wouldn't bring it to others. "May I ask you something, Sir?"

"Of course. But, you don't have to be so formal, please drop the 'Sir'."

"I found a gold brooch. At least I think it was gold. I found it close to where I live, where no one owns such fine jewelry."

He glanced at her, but it was too dark for her to read his expression. "That's strange," was all he said.

"I was afraid someone would think I'd stolen it and didn't dare to turn it in to the *verksmester*. I thought maybe it was the director's daughter who had lost it."

She had a feeling he was smiling in the dark. "Why is that?"

"She has rings on her fingers. I've seen it with my own eyes. I thought maybe it was her's, but she would never be walking on our street."

"What did you do with it? Did you turn it in to the police?"

"No, Johan was so kind and did it for me, but afterwards I was wondering...what if they don't find the owner...if...I mean..."

"You mean you wonder if you have any rights to it, since you were the one who found it."

"Yes, something like that."

"If the police find the owner he might be willing to pay a finder's reward. I assume that if nobody asks about it, it will be laying at the police station."

"Did you say a finder's reward?"

"Yes. If it's very valuable."

Elise imagined a handful of *kroner*. Maybe it would be enough for rent for several months, even food and firewood, maybe even a new skirt and a pair of shoes. Maybe she and Johan could get married this summer after all?

She was afraid he would read her mind and hurriedly changed the subject. "How long have you been in the Salvation Army?"

"For eight years, since 1897. Seven years after the Salvation Army came to Norway."

"Are you that old?!" She blurted out.

He laughed. "Don't I look it? I'm twenty-seven."

Elise thought quietly. If he had been a mill worker he would have looked older and worn out, his hands rough and rugged. "I heard you had a lot of resistance in the beginning. Mamma once said that often it was wild, out of control, especially at Grønland."

He laughed again; his laughter was good-natured and warm. "Yes, you can say that. Sometimes mobbing opponents stormed the platform and hit the trumpet players so hard that their teeth loosened and blood ran. A group was formed to get rid of the Salvation Army. Some of them wore blue sweaters with "Fight the Salvation Army" embroidered on their chests. Once they put dynamite under our building to blow it up in the air. That was before we moved to our meeting place at Pilestredet 22. But the belligerent attackers were converted and went to confession. Often we got bombarded with rotten eggs, mud, stones and dead rats. Yes, there were wild times."

Elise looked at him with curiosity. "And you still continued?"

She heard the smile in his voice when he replied, "When in your heart you truly believe in a cause, you don't give up, in spite of strong resistance. Besides, I had so many around me, people just as eager as I was. We knew we had to stand against scorn and mockery, even brutal violence. We were also aware it wasn't just the disorganized mobbing crowd who were against us, but also influential rich men who saw their interests threatened. But we didn't let that stop us. We had a battle to fight. A battle against cruel suffering, extreme poverty, vice and crimes in the shadows of the wealth of industrialization."

She looked directly at him, not understanding. "What did you mean by that?"

"You yourself are part of that. The industrialization led to poor folks leaving the countryside and coming to the city looking for work. They felt alienated, the work place was miserable, with poor lighting and no heat. The work day is too long. In addition to your twelve-hour day you are also forced to work overtime with no extra pay, and you get no vacation. The pay is so low you can't provide for a family. There is so much hunger and poverty, and for many, alcohol is the only comfort and escape from the exhausting, life draining, tiresome monotony of everyday life. While those on the top have become filthy rich. Now the factory owners are not all to blame. We can't judge all equally. Factory-owner Halvorsen, for example, he was one of our greatest supporters when the Salvation Army came to Norway."

"How many are you able to help?"

"Last year we gave out 6,345 cups or about 400 gallons of soup and 750 loaves of bread every week to the needy. There is so much poverty in this city. Just before I joined the Salvation Army, they started letting the homeless come into our hall at Grønland after the evening meeting was over. They were men who couldn't find work and didn't have roofs over their heads. On cold winter nights there could be up to three hundred."

"And now they live at the shelter in Urtegate," Elise said, thinking again about Pappa and what the Salvation Army soldier had said that for many alcohol was the only comfort and escape from the drudgery of everyday life. It sounded like he excused them. In any case, he seemed to understand why they drank.

But, why was it worse for Pappa than for Mamma? Why hadn't Hilda and she started drinking? Their workdays had been just as long as his; they had just as little to eat, and had frozen from the cold just as much as he had.

They had come to the foot of Akersbakken; she couldn't believe they were already there.

"Now I don't have far to go," he said, in his calm voice. "I rent a little room in the attic in one of the houses up there. Would you like me to walk you home?"

She shook her head. "No, thank you. I'm not scared anymore."

They continued in silence up the hill. He stopped under a street lamp and looked at her. "I hope you'll come back to the Temple often."

"Ja, I'll do that. As long as I can get help for Mamma. Thank you for walking with me, and thank you for the help."

He smiled that boyish smile again. "And thank you!" he replied. "That's why I am there. To help others. If you need me, you can contact someone in the Salvation Army and ask for Emanuel Ringstad."

Elise thanked him again and started to run. Her steps were lighter. I'm excited about telling Johan that maybe we can get a finder's reward for the brooch, she thought, and was the happiest she'd felt in a long time.

Chapter 14

Most of windows were dark when she got home. She ran into the backyard and looked up at Johan's kitchen window to see if he was still up. To her joy she saw light. She hurried and ran up the steps.

He opened the door immediately when she knocked, obviously happy to see her. "I'm glad you're here, Elise. I have got so much to tell you," he said eagerly.

"Me too," she replied as he wrapped his arms around her.

"Mamma has gone to bed," he whispered in her ear.

She smiled and leaned her head into his broad, warm chest. He lifted her face towards his and without a moment's hesitation his lips were on hers.

"You should have been a fly on the wall at the meeting tonight, Elise," he said enthusiastically as he let go of her and pulled her towards the kitchen table. "The guys were more fired-up than ever. Many think we should go out on strike!"

"Strike?" Elise frowned. "Isn't that dangerous?"

"Not if there are enough of us. What would the factory owners do without us? Without the workers, the machines come to a stand-still and nothing gets done, no goods to sell and no income. They are completely dependent on us, Elise."

"But, I remember what Agnes' father said about the workers at Kværner Factory when they…"

"That was something completely different," he interrupted. "They only made noise and threw rocks at Onsum's house. The police had to use clubs and sticks to get rid of them. That's how it was when the brickyard workers stormed the owner's home, too. They broke his windows, and trampled down his garden."

Elise nodded. "They were sentenced to one year hard labor."

"But that's not the way we're talking about doing it," Johan was so eager he stumbled over his words. "Have you heard about the match-girls? Three hundred girls, many not older than seven or eight years old, marched all the way on foot, about 5 miles, from Etterstad to Karl Johansgate. At the front of the parade, they carried two big white banners with red letters: "We demand only 1 *øre* more per gross and better sanitary conditions." The folks who saw it gasped in astonishment and disgust. That same evening there was a meeting in Torggate. A doctor showed them two girls with severe phosphorus burns. The one had a swollen bulge covering half her face and most of the face of the other girl was gone. She had surgery and would look like that the rest of her life. That was when folks first knew about the insane working conditions. And the danger!"

"But, we're not like that," Elise protested.

"No, maybe we haven't lost half of our faces, but our pay has been cut even lower and folks can't afford to eat anything but *grøt* and *velling*. And freezing, that's something we all know. Fru Evertsen soaks her morning piece of bread in moonshine because it warms up her whole body she says. Moonshine is the only thing that is cheap. There is a moonshine keg on the counter in every store, and parents send their kids to get a jug so they can unwind after a hard day. Is it any wonder so many turn into drunkards? I don't mean we should fight, Elise. I mean we should do like the match-girls, stop working and go in a peaceful demonstration march. We don't have to ask for much, just a little more in our pay envelope each week so we have enough for food and heat."

Elise was still skeptical. "I remember what Agnes' father told us about the workers who walked in a protest parade and demonstrated on behalf of the street-girls. Several thousand workers demonstrated, not for themselves, but for the unfortunate girls who were forced to sell their bodies to survive. When they marched past the Stiftsgården where the prime minister lived, and lowered their banners in salute, he didn't even come out. The curtains were pulled shut in all the windows."

"Do you mean that we should give up because they didn't succeed?"

"No, but…" She sighed. "It's just the way it is, Johan. The rich live in one world, we live in another. It's always been like that."

Johan shook his head and looked at her in frustration.

Elise was sitting on his lap. She thought it would be best to slide off and sit on the other stool. "Don't get mad, Johan. I'm just afraid you'll get into something you shouldn't. We're lucky. We have work. Think about all those sleeping on the floor in the shelter at Grønland, satisfied to get a scrap of food once a day. And think about all those who have to share a kitchen with another family. In Valborg's house they have divided the kitchen with a line on the floor, and mercy be to him who dares to cross that line! And think of all who must live on the streets begging to survive. We don't have to."

Johan got up and got the coffee kettle. Without asking, he poured a *kaffeskvett* for both of them and added a spoonful of sugar.

"I've been to the Temple," she said, to change the subject. She understood that he was disappointed that she wasn't more interested. But she had enough to worry about. She didn't need to get involved in politics, as well.

Johan sipped his coffee, looking down at the table without replying.

"Something good happened there," she continued and looked at him in suspense, but he didn't seem to be listening.

"Did you know there is something called a finder's reward?"

Johan still didn't answer; he seemed deeply engrossed in his own thoughts.

"Maybe the owner of the brooch will put up a poster saying that whoever finds it will receive a reward of ten *kroner* if they turn it in. Or maybe five," she added, ashamed of her greediness.

Johan quickly lifted his head and turned his attention to her, "What are you talking about?"

Elise suddenly felt small. She understood that a finder's reward was too much to hope for. "One of the Salvation Army soldiers told me that," she tried to excuse herself.

"You told him about the brooch?"

"I said it only to a Salvation Army soldier, they don't gossip."

"Why in…" He stopped and held the words back. "Why in the world would you tell him about the brooch when you don't have it anymore?"

Elise felt her face turning red. "He lives in Akersbakken and we walked home together. He was so easy to talk with and understood how difficult it's been for me, thinking about how Pappa fell in the river and froze to death. After the meeting he talked with one of the slum sisters who promised to bring Hilda some boots and to look in on Mamma."

"But why did you tell him about the brooch? You who didn't dare tell the director or go to the police because you were scared they would think you'd stolen it!"

Elise looked down. "He was so knowledgeable, and he said whatever I told him would stay between him and me."

She didn't dare look at him. Johan had taken the responsibility. Why did she have to babble to others about it?

"What did you tell him we had done with the brooch?"

"I only told him you had delivered it for me."

"You talked about *me*, too?"

In a flash she realized that he was jealous, and she enjoyed feeling she was special.

"I didn't say anything other than that we are engaged." She glanced up at him. "Don't be upset, Johan. You would have thought he was a good man, too, if you had met him. Maybe Hilda will get new boots. Well, not new, but with no holes in the soles. Did you know the Salvation Army gives out over four hundred gallons of soup to the needy every week? And seven hundred and fifty loaves of bread?"

"So, you see how much poverty there is. And how low the wages are."

She nodded, but refused to give him the upper hand. "He's only twenty-seven, but he's been in the Salvation Army for eight years. I'm sure he could have become a minister or a doctor, but instead he wants to spend his life helping others."

"So, it was a young man who walked you home tonight...Strange that he took care of you, when certainly there were at least fifty or a hundred other girls at the meeting, all just as starving and frozen."

Elise giggled. "I knew it! You're jealous!" She looked at him teasingly.

For a moment it seemed Johan would get angry, but then his face lit up with a big smile. He came over to her, threw his arms around her and hugged her close into him. "Yes, I'm jealous. At every man who looks at you. I want you all to myself. Nobody is allowed to walk you home and you are not allowed to share your concerns with anyone but me."

She smiled and leaned her head against his warm, strong body. "I don't want that either, Johan. I don't want anyone else but you. Next time you'll have to come with me to the Temple, and then I won't have to be walked home by eager, young men."

"Come here." He wrapped his arms around her again. His voice dropped to a deep whisper, "Now I can touch you a little."

She felt warm when she cuddled in his arms and liked the way his hand fumbled around. "I wish we could be like this all night," she whispered against his lips.

"If you run up and let your mother know that you're home, you can sneak back later when they're all sleeping."

"You mean, stay here all night?"

"Why not? You're always the last one to bed. The others won't even notice you're not on your mattress. Then you can sneak back up into the kitchen in the morning and pretend you've just gotten up."

"But what if your mother...?"

He firmly shook his head. "When you stand twelve hours a day in the factory, you don't lay awake at night."

Elise felt a tingling sensation run through her body. "But we can't..."

"No, my silly girl. I won't touch you. Well, at least not more than I already have."

"But, can you handle that, Johan? Remember how it was up in the meadow last summer."

He chuckled and gently kissed her cheek. "Since I managed that time, I'll be able to again."

"You must promise me. It's enough with Hilda..."

"Ja, I promise," he added and put his hand inside her shirt, as if to show her how far he would go.

Elise closed her eyes and giggled. It was so good to feel his warm, gentle hand holding her breast. "I'll be right back," she whispered, getting up quickly and quietly opening the door. She ran up the steps two at a time.

Chapter 15

She was halfway up when she stopped and listened. It sounded like crying coming from the kitchen. Her throat tightened. Could something have happened with Mamma? Had she...? Her thoughts ran wild. "Dear God," she begged, "don't let anything have happened. Not tonight."

She shouldn't have gone away and left Mamma, it wasn't more than two days since Pappa had drowned. She shouldn't have talked and laughed with the young Salvation Army soldier, and she should have gone right up, shouldn't have stopped to see Johan. She'd taken "all the time in the world" with him and agreed to come back and be with him tonight. How could she? If something happened to Mamma tonight, she would never forgive herself.

But then she remembered that she had gone to ask for new boots for Hilda and if one of the slum sisters could come to Mamma. Hopefully, God would understand why she'd been gone so long.

She went up the steps with reluctance and fear. She *could* not, she *would* not, she *wasn't ready* to go in and find Mamma lying lifeless in bed. Her face jaundiced like Pappa's with stiff fingers folded in an unnatural way. No, no one could expect that of her. Not tonight. Not when it'd had only been a short while since she had been to Storgata 40 and identified Pappa. God could not be that heartless.

Her body seemed as heavy as lead, and her legs almost slipped out from under her as she took the last steps toward the door.

The crying continued. It was Peder. She imagined Kristian sitting there, a dark and hard look on his face, like a grown-up man. He didn't cry. Not even when his father died only two days ago. What was it he had said yesterday? "It don't bother me none. I never saw 'im anyway."

Suddenly she heard something that sent shivers down her spine. Someone was laughing. Kristian.

She was ready to storm into the kitchen in anger, but instead quiet composure came over her. She must have misunderstood. Mamma was okay, nothing had happened to her.

Eagerly she opened the door.

Peder stood sobbing, his face bright red. He was in the furthest corner and Kristian was howling with laughter.

"Haven't you gone to bed yet?" Elise knew she should be harder on them, but with the relief of knowing it was not Mamma, it was impossible to be angry.

"Peder got bit in the butt!"

Elise wrinkled her brow, not understanding, looked over at her little brother. He lowered his head in humiliation.

"He forgot to kick the outhouse door to scare the rats away," Kristian said, grinning.

Now Elise felt a surge of rage, "And you stand there laughing?! *Fy*! Shame on you. You're a brat! What if it had been you?"

"Hah!" He cockily shrugged his shoulders and boasted, "Do ya really think they would'a dared?"

Elise ignored him and went over to Peder. "Let me see, Peder."

"No!" He shook his head.

"I have to take a look to be able to help you. If you've been bitten I have to put something on it so you don't get an infection."

Reluctantly he pulled his pants down, turned his back to her and let her examine it.

Elise took the iodine from the tin box up on the shelf, and Peder screamed loudly. Afterwards, she poured a little watered-down beer and sugar in a mug and handed it to him. He drank it eagerly.

"Now, go to bed right away. It's late and you have to get up early tomorrow for school."

Peder stood still and looked up at her, "Are you going to bed, too, Elise?"

"I hadn't planned to quite yet. Do you know where Hilda is?"

"Out running around as usual," Kristian said contempt in his voice.

"Elise?" Peder looked up at her pleadingly. "Can't you go to bed, you, too?"

Elise was just about to say something, but his pleading eyes stopped her. "Go in the *kammers*, Kristian. I want to have a few words with Peder."

Kristian obeyed and Elise stood by Peder. Waiting.

Peder looked down, wiggling his toes. "It's just dat…I'm so scared dat Mamma…"

Elise gently combed her fingers through his hair. "I'll come lay down with you, Peder."

He lifted his face and looked at her; relief filled his big, blue eyes.

"I just have to go to outhouse first," she added quickly.

"Kick da door first, den, Elise."

"Don't worry, I'll do that! Get undressed now, my little friend, Peder."

When she came down to the second floor, she knocked softly on the door so Johan's mother wouldn't hear her.

Johan was standing right by the door. She saw he had combed his hair. "Elise," he whispered.

"I can't come tonight, Johan. Peder's not feeling well."
She didn't dare tell him the truth about the rat bite, afraid
he'd laugh, too. But that wasn't the only reason.

He was about to protest, but instead his shoulders sank
and he took a deep breath, "You can't?"

"I can come another night. He'll be okay soon."

He nodded, not wanting to show how disappointed he
was, but she could see it anyway.

She turned away quickly, afraid he would try to talk her
out of it. The temptation to stay was hard to resist.

A little later when she crawled into bed, Hilda still hadn't
come home. What was it with that girl? She who had always
been so well-behaved, obedient to Mamma, responsible and
kind. She seemed suddenly bewitched. One would almost
think she was madly in love; some are so infatuated that they
forget everything around them, but she couldn't be that much
in love with the middle-aged, repulsive *verksmester* could
she? Or was it Lorang, the errand boy? Could it be she hadn't
told him she was pregnant?

"Elise?" Peder whispered to her in the dark.

"Yes, what is it?"

"Don't ya t'ink Mamma looked a little odd?"

"No different than usual. She was sleeping calmly when I
went and looked at her."

"She din't want no food."

"She eats like a bird, Peder. One doesn't need much
laying in bed day in and day out."

"Ya t'ink Pappa can see us now?"

"Ja, he's sitting up in heaven, looking down on us, proud
of having such great kids."

"Maybe he's regrettin' usin' all 'is money on moonshine
and not on us."

"I'm sure he is."

It was quiet and still in the narrow little bed.

"Elise?"

"Now go to sleep, Peder. You need to get up early."

"Did ya know da Rodeløkka boys got into a fist-fight wid da Sagene gang again?"

Elise yawned. "No, I didn't know that."

"It's kinda scary goin' to school, not knowin' when dey all of a sudden can pop up."

"Don't you walk with Kristian?"

"Kristian says he ain't walkin' wid little kids."

"Little kids, hmmmm. He's only one year older than you. I'll talk with him, Peder, but now you have to go to sleep."

"*Natta*, Elise. I'm so glad you're here, I am."

Even though it was quiet and Peder's deep breathing signaled that he finally was asleep, her thoughts wouldn't stop. How could she marry Johan when Peder was so afraid and didn't trust anyone but her? Mamma was too weak to take care of them, and Hilda had started running around. And Kristian couldn't be trusted. No, she couldn't get married. She was obligated to live at home.

Below on the next floor, Johan lay suppressing his disappointment. How many disappointments would he tolerate before he would give up?

The following day, when Elise came home during her lunch break a woman Salvation Army officer was standing by the entryway gate. It looked as if she waited for someone, and Elise guessed she was coming to them.

"Elise Løvlien?"

Elise nodded and smiled.

The woman reached out her hand. "Captain Maren Sørby. I understand your mother is sick and you need help."

Elise noticed she was carrying a basket with something in it and prayed a silent prayer that it was boots for Hilda, even though Hilda didn't deserve them right now. She hadn't come home before Elise got up this morning. It wouldn't help anyone if Hilda got tuberculosis, too.

She went ahead of the Salvation Army officer up to the third level. When she opened the door, suddenly she became aware of how wretched and dismal the kitchen looked. For the first time, she saw it through a stranger's eyes, saw things she otherwise didn't think about. A huge cockroach raced across the kitchen table, the curtains had holes and the wall around the woodstove was covered in soot. She should have washed down the whole room, but was too exhausted in the evening. Washing clothes, scrubbing the steps and patching the boys' clothes were more important.

"Please come in," she mumbled and nodded to the kitchen stool, feeling ashamed and embarrassed.

The woman sat down. She was just as pale and frail as many of the workers, Elise thought, but something about her attitude was different. She looked gratified and satisfied. Elise didn't understand how anyone could like trudging between the filthy homes of folks plagued in poverty, dealing with quarrelsome drunks, screaming kids, stench and bedbugs.

"You have only your lunch break so do what you need to do, even if I'm here," she said in a kind voice.

Elise started stoking the fire in the woodstove.

"I should greet you from Captain Emanuel Ringstad. He was at the Sagene slum station this morning."

Elise, irritated with herself, was aware she was blushing and was glad her back was turned to the woman.

"He told me all about your difficult situations."

He hopefully didn't tell about the brooch. Elise was terrified. Johan definitely wouldn't like that.

"Tell me, are you sure your mother has tuberculosis. Has the doctor been here?"

Elise shook her head. "Mamma will not have him here. She doesn't like him." Elise stopped, appalled by what she'd just said. What if the slum sister knew the doctor? Besides it wasn't true. Elise had a feeling there was something else behind her mother's refusal. As long as the doctor hadn't been there, she could hold on to the hope it wasn't tuberculosis. The worst would be to hear the doctor say, "Nothing can be done, there's no hope."

"But you are well aware of how contagious tuberculosis is? You've no doubt heard that it's called "the white pest." When one member of the family has gotten it, there's a high risk that all will get it."

Elise nodded. "But in the case of Magda on the Corner, only the big sister has it and the rest of the kids are always up in her bed."

The slum sister nodded. "Yes, that's what is so strange about it. It's like the illness strikes completely at random. In some families everyone dies, while others in the same stairwell aren't affected at all. Is your mother vomiting blood?"

Elise shook her head. "She has a constant fever, is pale and clammy in her face, and sometimes has inflamed red blotches on her cheeks. When she wakes up in the morning, she's wringing wet with sweat. It's been like this for several months. She first started coughing last summer."

"This has been going on several months, since last summer?" The slum sister's eyes widened in alarm. She stood up from the stool. "Can I go in to her?"

Elise nodded, relieved that finally someone would see Mamma, but at the same time afraid of the answer. She opened the *kammers* door and stuck her head in. "Mamma, there is a slum sister here who wants to say hello to you."

Mamma lay in bed in the same position as always and weakly moved her head.

Elise turned to the slum sister who pulled a pair of shiny polished boots from her basket. "Tell her I brought these for your sister," she whispered.

"She brought Hilda some new boots. Hilda's feet are soaking wet every day, her old boots have big holes in them."

Mamma opened her eyes and looked up at her. "Ask her to come in," she said weakly.

While the slum sister was in the *kammers* with Mamma, Elise cooked up *velling* and prayed to God that the sickness wasn't tuberculosis.

Finally Elise heard footsteps coming across the floor and in the next second the door opened. The slum sister looked very serious. Carefully closing the door behind her, she shook her head and whispered: "I'm afraid your mother has tuberculosis, Elise. Your instincts were right."

Elise shook her head; she had known it all along. It was different, though, hearing it from a stranger who had seen it before and knew the symptoms. A cold chill went through her body, tears stuck in her throat, and she shook with fear. She turned to the stove, vigorously stirring the *velling*.

"I'll try to find more nourishing food for her, and you have to start boiling the silverware and dishes so the rest of you won't be infected. The best would be if she could be admitted to Grefsen Tuberculosis Sanatorium, but it's private and much too expensive for folks with low wages."

Finally Elise managed to turn and look at her, her lips quivering. "How long can she..." She bit her lips to hold back the tears. "How long does it normally take?"

The slum sister shook her head. "It's impossible to say. It can take a long time, or it can go fast. I heard your father passed away recently. Was he sick, too?"

Elise shook her head. "He slid on the ice and drowned. During the night last Saturday."

"Was it really *that* recent?" Her voice sounded surprised. "Then there hasn't been a funeral yet?"

Elise shook her head again.

The slum sister grasped her basket and pulled out a paper bag. "I brought a loaf of bread for you. I'll try to come by as often as possible, but there are so desperately many others in the same situation. The worst of all is where the father is drinking and the mother has died. All those orphaned children, you know."

Elise nodded. "Don't worry about us. We'll manage."

"You have a sister, is that right?"

"Yes, Hilda is sixteen and works at the spinning mill, too, where I work."

"It's so good there are two of you. Then you're probably able to support your mother and your brothers."

Elise didn't say anything. She couldn't tell her that Hilda was pregnant and had started staying out all night. That shame they'd keep to themselves. Hilda also had a fever lately. If she had been infected by Mamma, she wouldn't be able to work much longer.

"Goodbye, Elise. I'll pray for you all."

Elise nodded without saying anything.

The slum sister had just disappeared down the steps when Elise heard quick footsteps coming up. Johan burst in, his face red after running all the way from Seilduken, happiness and warmth in his eyes. He threw his arms around her before she knew what was happening!

"Tonight you can come down," he whispered eagerly in her ear. "Mamma said she met Peder in the steps on his way to school this morning, and he was obviously feeling okay again."

Elise didn't respond. She closed her eyes and clutched him. "Mamma has tuberculosis," she whispered, fighting back the tears.

"You have known that for a long time."

"Ja, but I was hoping maybe..." She sobbed, forcing out the words, "and Hilda is out all night, Peder is afraid Mamma will die and Kristian refuses to walk with him to school."

"There, there, Elise. It's not like you to give up. Kristian is like most boys his age. It's embarrassing to have a little brother tagging along. That Hilda is gone all night isn't so strange, either, now that she's pregnant with her boyfriend's baby. And now they don't have to worry about having an accident." He laughed gently, caressing her cheek.

A sharp jolt shot through Elise. Johan still thought it was Lorang who was the father of the baby Hilda was carrying. She felt it was almost a betrayal to let him be tricked like this, but she couldn't tell him. Not yet.

"It's only you who's so careful," Johan continued. "Take a trip up to the The Crib; you'll see how many have done the same as Hilda."

"I thought we agreed to wait until we're married."

"And that's only five months away!" He lifted her up and swung her around. "Five months, Elise! Then you are mine! Think of it!"

His words were music to her ears. She imagined lying nearly naked in his arms, tight against his strong, warm body. There would be no more freezing cold nights - impossible to sleep. Soon she would always be warm and safe.

He pulled her onto his lap and planted kisses on her mouth - nonstop. The anxiety lessened, her body relaxed and warmth came back.

Maybe she could steal away and go down to Johan tonight after Peder fell asleep. If not the whole night, at least for a little while. Snuggle close to him, lean against him and absorb energy from the strength of his strong body. They would smother each other with kisses until they couldn't breathe anymore. He could touch her, at least a little, and when he got overly passionate, like up in the meadow last summer, she'd remind him that it was only five months until summer again.

"Don't worry! It'll work out, Elise," he whispered in a low husky voice, like last night. "It's doesn't have to be tuberculosis, though."

"The slum sister said it is."

He drew his head back a little. "A slum sister was here?"

"Ja. She left just before you came. I thought maybe you had run into her in the stairwell."

"Did she *say* it was tuberculosis?" He seemed surprised, even if he tried to hide it.

"Ja, she thought so. She did ask if Mamma is spitting up blood, and she's not."

"There you see. Then it's not absolutely certain it's tuberculosis. Is she going to help you?"

"She said she would try to drop by every now and then. She brought a loaf of bread and a pair of boots for Hilda."

Johan smiled. "Don't you see, Elise? Things work out better than we think. Your mother will get some help, and you won't have to worry about her when you are at the spinning mill."

"She didn't know how often she could come by. She said there are so many who need help. Many have it much worse than us."

He kissed her neck. "I'm sure she'll come by every day. It's easier to help people who are kind to each other, and it's hard to find someone who's as kind to their mother as you are. Now cheer up, Elise. We have each other; we have nothing to complain about."

She smiled at him. "I'll come down tonight after Peder has fallen asleep," she whispered.

He smiled and sighed. "I don't know how I'll ever be able to wait…"

Chapter 16

The rest of the day was going quickly, Elise thought. Johan had talked out of her melancholy mood; she looked forward to this evening, and told herself it didn't have to be true that Mamma had tuberculosis. When the slum sister comes with nourishing food, when its springtime and the windows are open and the room is aired out, Mamma will no doubt be better. When summer comes, she'll probably be well enough to be in the wedding celebration.

The thought filled her body with warm yearnings.

Before going down to Johan tonight, she would have a serious word with Hilda. Tell her she expected her to stay home at night. If she wouldn't listen, she could threaten to tell Johan the name of the baby's father. Hilda had a special respect for Johan, which would make her think twice. Besides she shouldn't be out running around now only a few days before Pappa's funeral. The black shawl she'd borrowed from Fru Evertsen had to be darned and Kristian's wool socks had holes again.

But what if Hilda discovered she herself wasn't in the *kammers* tonight. What would she say? Ja, there's a saying "if you live in a glass house, don't throw stones."

But, *she* hadn't been out any other nights. And she would only be down with Johan, and could run up if something happened. She wouldn't go before Peder and the others were asleep.

The factory siren howled, just as shrill and horrible as always.

In the middle of the bridge, she saw Hilda in front of her. Well, it was impossible to separate her from the other darkly clad figures, their shawls wrapped tightly around their heads and shoulders, but she knew it was Hilda by her laughter. To think that she was laughing, now, before Pappa was in the ground.

"Hilda?"

Her sister turned around. "Wha' is it?"

"I have to talk to you."

"Is it so terribly urgent?"

Then Elise saw that Hilda was walking with Valborg. It was dangerous to get too close to Valborg, Elise thought. Everything that was said would spread like wildfire over all of Sagene as soon as they turned their backs.

"Mamma had a visit from one of the slum sisters today."

"Huff," said Valborg, contempt in her voice. "Mamma says the Salvation Army ain't nothin' but humbug. It's the devil's work she says. Women can't be leaders, ever'body knows that, an' ya can't call 'em officers, either. War ain't for women-folk she says. They wave their hankies in the air, clappin' their hands and shoutin' 'allelujah and amen ever' other sentence, as if *that* puts bread on our tables."

Elise was irritated. She stopped and her voice was sharp. "They give out many hundred loaves of bread to the poor every week."

"How'dya know that?"

"I went to the Temple last night."

"And they was praisin' themselves?"

"Absolutely not. They told how they would continue fighting as long as there are poor folks on this earth, as long as there are children crying and as long as there are street-girls and drunks."

"Too bad they didn't 'elp your Pa then, Elise. Or was he too filthy and ragged for them to take 'im in."

Elise had to catch her breath. She knew she shouldn't get hissy over Valborg, she was just that way and had always been, but she couldn't let it go.

"What a terrible thing to say! He was our father after all!"

"But, he was always staggerin' around dead drunk in da streets, and he beat up bot' you and your Ma.

"That was just the last two years. Before that, when he worked at Seilduken..."

"Shut up!" Hilda yelled. "Do you have to talk about Pappa? He ain't here anymore. There is nothin' to discuss."

Valborg stuck her arm in Hilda's. "Come, Hilda."

Just then, one of Valborg's girlfriends showed up. "I saw ya out last night, Elise," she said in a bantering voice. "I t'ought you were wit' Johan, but wow was I wrong."

Valborg stopped abruptly and shifted her eyes from her girlfriend to Elise and back to her girlfriend. "What are ya talkin' about?"

"Elise was flutterin' around out on da town last night, with a Salvation Army soldier."

"Huffda?" Valborg heard in disbelief. "Is it true, Elise?"

"Stop that foolishness. Why would I do that when I'm engaged to Johan?"

Valborg's girlfriend flamed up. "You are lyin'! I saw you wit' my own eyes, when you crossed Ullevaalsveien and went up Akersbakken."

"I was at the Temple – to get *you* new boots, Hilda," she sputtered out in angry words. "The Salvation Army soldier was going the same way and offered to walk with me. Is that fluttering around out on the town?"

"You are lyin' again! I snuk after ya, and ya stood a long time under da street lamp. He smiled so affectionately. He even gave you 'is name, 'e did! I 'ave never met one in the Salvation Army who told me 'is name."

Elise didn't bother to reply. What was the use? No matter what she said, they'd twist it around. They were envious: Valborg because of Johan, and her girlfriend because of the Salvation Army soldier. Maybe Valborg's girlfriend had seen him before and followed because she was infatuated with him.

She hurried quickly away from them, and got home long before Hilda.

As soon as she got into the kitchen, she set a kettle of water on the woodstove to get warm soapy water for the scrub bucket. I have to scrub this rage out of me! She thought pursing her lips tightly. That witch Valborg! And her cursed girlfriend! Big blabber mouths, gossipers, nosey and cruel. She blended lye in the wash water, took a hard grip on the scrub brush and attacked the kitchen floor. When the slum sister comes the next time, she'll know from the smell that it had a good scrubbing since the last time.

"Whads'witcha?" Kristian asked, irritated when the water splashed up on his legs. He and Peder sat doing school lessons.

"Something stinks."

"Has the outhouse man been here and emptied it today?"

"I'm not talking about that kind of stink. Do your school lessons now. It's your turn to get water and firewood."

She heard a noise in the hallway and Hilda came in. "Jeeze. What's with you?! You were in a heck of a hurry today."

Elise straightened her back. "I'd like to have a couple serious words with you!"

"You're not my mother!"

"Oh, be happy I'm not! Where were you last night?"

Hilda took off her shawl and hung it on the nail on the wall. "Where are the boots you talked about?"

"You won't get them until you tell me where you were last night."

"It wasn't you who got them."

"Ja, that's right. But if I hadn't gone to the Temple last night, there'd be no boots for you."

Hilda's eyes shifted uneasily, and shot a glance at Peder and Kristian. "I'm not saying anything as long as they are sitting here."

"Peder, Kristian. Out!"

Peder lifted his head and looked in alarm up at Elise. "Out? You told us we 'ave to do our school lessons."

"You only need to go out in the stairwell for a bit while Hilda confesses something."

They dragged their feet reluctantly towards the door.

As soon as they left, Elise turned to her sister, "Okay, now you've got to confess!"

Hilda looked down. "I was at the factory." Then she lifted her chin, as if she realized she had no reason to be ashamed. "Why are you making such an issue out if it? You know who I'm with."

"*Verksmester?*" Elise glared at her in disbelief. "Are you still seeing Herr Paulsen?"

Hilda nodded with a triumphant glow. "We slept in his office."

"Oh, I'm sure you slept alright." Elise heard the scorn in her voice.

Hilda sneered.

Elise felt a flash of rage. "How can you do such a terrible thing to yourself? With that middle-aged, fat…"

She didn't get any further. Hilda's hand flew at Elise with a cracking slap across her cheek. "Shut up!" She yelled.

179

"He's nice, he is. He gives me cakes and chocolate, and treats me like a princess. He says I'm the prettiest girl he's ever met. And it doesn't even bother him that I'm pregnant. Quite the opposite. He's happy about it."

Elise stared at her, mouth wide open. "He's happy about it?"

Hilda lifted her head and looked haughtily straight into Elise's eyes, "Yes, he is!"

Elise squinted at her again, in disbelief, "But…but…"

"I know what you're thinking, but you can just forget that. It ain't worse for me than all the others. It's just to close my eyes and think of something else."

Elise felt shame burning her cheeks. Hilda was acting like a street-girl. She had given the *verksmester* her body for cakes and chocolate! Oh Lord, what a miserable mess!

Kristian banged on the door. "Can we come in now? We're freezing!"

Elise didn't reply. The boys stormed through the door.

She went back to scrubbing the floor, but felt like the wind had been knocked out of her. Thinking about what Hilda had done mulled around in her head. What would they tell Mamma? Sooner or later Mamma would know and demand to know the name of the baby's father.

They had to come up with something. Pretend it was Lorang, the errand boy, or another of the guys in the street. It was different when it was two who loved each other, would probably get married after a while, have the baby baptized and could look at the minister with heads held high.

She glanced over at her sister. Hilda had gotten the package with the boots and sat on the stool, lacing them up. They were well worn, Elise could see that now, but polished and had no holes. One or two sizes too big, but that was better than too small. They could make paper soles from old newspapers to fill them up.

Hilda looked up, her eyes gleamed. "Look how nice they are. Can you imagine how envious Valborg will be?"

Elise stood still and pondered, looking at Hilda. Hilda had already forgotten what they had talked about only a second ago. The boots were more important. She shook her head hopelessly. Sixteen years old, Elise thought, already working full time, but not mature, not for a long time yet.

To her relief Hilda went to bed at the same time as Peder and Kristian. No wonder, Elise thought, she who'd spent last night in the *verksmester's* office while Elise was busy taking care of Mamma.

She sensed that Mamma knew something, her eyes questioned, but she didn't say anything. "Wasn't it great that the slum sister was here?" Elise asked trying to get her to think about something else.

Mamma looked at her with tear filled eyes. "It's too late, Elise," she whispered. "Everything is too late."

Elise glanced quickly over at the boys, but they were busy undressing and arguing over who would sleep next to the wall. She shook her head. "She didn't say that to me. She was glad you aren't coughing up blood, and wasn't so sure you have tuberculosis. When you get better food, and when it's no longer so biting cold, we can open the windows and let in the fresh air. You'll feel a lot better. Next summer you can sit outside on a bench by the bridge and get some sun in your face. That helps, they say. It's the hard winters that break folks down."

Mamma was quiet, but Elise saw a slight hope in her eyes.

After she'd finished with Mamma, and the boys were in bed, she sat down by the kitchen table to darn socks. She had to be sure everyone was sleeping. She wouldn't stay long down with Johan. Mamma could wake up and need help. Often Peder had nightmares and was scared. Johan, who had a sick sister, must understand how difficult it was for her to be away from all this. Especially for the whole night.

Her thoughts returned to Hilda. She just couldn't comprehend the fact that Hilda had done this of her own free will. If it had been a young man Hilda was in love with, she could easily understand. She thought of Johan and herself, how passionate they had been, when the sun warmed their skin last summer and they laid alone together, with only the fluffy clouds and Sunday and birds twittering around them. Just the thought sparked fire to smolder in her whole body. Her insides quivered with excitement! But, with a middle-aged, fat man like the *verksmester*? With fat fingers, thinning hair and old-man's breath? What help was it to close her eyes and think about something else, she had to *notice* it?!

She remembered something one of the spinning girls had told once. It was during lunch break before Mamma got sick, and Elise had stayed at the spinning mill. Several of the girls put their heads together, listening with saucer-size eyes. The spinning girl told what she had seen in the forest when she was out picking blueberries the Sunday before. She had heard some strange noises, moaning and groaning. Suddenly she discovered two people rolling around in the heather; a big burly, old man laying on top of a young girl. The spinning girl had thought at first she was witnessing a murder and stood still with fright. Then she saw the young girl pull up her frock, and untie her underpants, while the old man fumbled with his belt buckle and fly and pulled it out. The spinning girl was shocked - it was so huge. She wanted to turn and run away, but was afraid they'd hear her. Instead she stood there, watching. She'd shuddered. "Then the strangest thing happened," she said. "The young girl wasn't crying, rather the opposite. She was lying there smiling, pulling her legs wider apart and looking like she really enjoyed it!"

Elise waved that revolting memory aside. No way did she believe Hilda had lain there smiling, helping him and actually enjoying it.

Now Johan sat down in the kitchen and waited. Impatiently. Happy. He was almost always happy. That was one of his best traits. Would Hilda ever experience such a handsome and generous boyfriend, after she had botched up as she had? What man would marry someone who acted like a street-girl?

She finished one sock, put the needle and darning thread aside and got up from the table. It had been quiet in the *kammers* for a while now. She stood quietly and listened, draped her shawl around her shoulders and tip-toed out.

It was silent over all. The whole *gård* slept.

She went noiselessly down the steps, didn't knock on the door, but opened it quietly, as Johan had told her to do.

He sat reading an old newspaper from Fru Berg, a neighbor, who usually gave them to him after she'd read them. He looked up when he heard her opening the door. His face broke out in a warm, welcoming smile. He held his pointer finger in front of his mouth, and beckoned her to him.

She sat down close beside him, slipped her arms around his waist and snuggled into him. They nestled in each other's arms several minutes, so happy to be together. He pointed toward the corner in the kitchen, and Elise noticed he had put a pillow and a blanket on the floor.

"Come," he whispered. "Let's lay down for a while."

Then both the bobbin-girl's story and Hilda's shame came over her. She bit her lips, hesitated.

"Don't dilly-dally, Elise. I won't hurt you."

He blew out the lamp.

It felt so unbelievably good to be in his arms, feel his warmth, enjoy the smells of both tobacco and a man, and know he loved her just as much as she loved him. His lips were warm and firm, and although his hands were big and strong, they were light as a feather when they glided gently over her body.

"I was so scared you wouldn't come." He whispered. "I love you so much, Elise, more and more every day."

She eagerly pressed her body into his. She couldn't get close enough. "Next summer, Johan... I'll be in your arms every night."

"And I'll kiss you and kiss you until you're all out of breath."

She cooed, "We won't be getting much sleep."

"Ja, because we'll be doing even more." He put his hand inside her shirt, slowly caressing her naked skin. "Do you like it?" he whispered softly.

"Hmmmm."

He took her hand, guided it down, to the huge, hard bump that throbbed in anticipation.

He was breathing hard. Elise got scared. She pulled her hand away. "We can't, Johan."

"Only a little," he begged, whispering with burning passion in her ear.

"No, we can't. I'm dreading what I have to tell you, maybe you'll understand why we can't."

He pulled back, and she immediately regretted what she'd said. She could have waited a little.

"What is it?" he asked, his voice was anxious. He who was not easily rattled!

"It's Hilda."

She heard him take a deep breath. Hesitant. "What is it now?!"

"It's not Lorang, the errand boy, like you think." She had decided to tell Johan the truth. Sooner or later he'd find out anyway, and now she needed his help. She wouldn't let Hilda's anger stand in the way; besides Hilda needn't find out what Johan knew. "Promise not to tell a living soul."

'Of course, I promise, if it's that important to you."

"It's the *verksmester*."

Silence fell over him. He was so quiet that Elise began to worry. He propped himself up on his elbows. The room was dark, but she felt his rage. "Herr Paulsen?!" he gasped in disbelief.

"Ja."

She had a feeling he was making a fist. "I'll make him pay for it, I swear!" He was about to get up, but Elise held him back. "It's not what you think, Johan. Hilda did it of her own free will."

He breathed a deep, long disgusting groan.

"Now I don't believe my own ears! I can't believe what I'm hearing! Do you mean to tell me Hilda went to bed with the *verksmester* willingly?"

"Ja, she told me herself. She wasn't even embarrassed," Elise clenched with shame.

"Does he know…?"

"Yes, he has promised to take care of it. Whatever he means by that, I don't know. But I think he plans to support Hilda and the baby in some way. Maybe not with a lot of money, but…"

"No! He rose up. Now I've got to go have a smoke. This is the worst I have ever heard."

He got up, fumbled his way to the kitchen table and lit the kerosene lamp.

Elise joined him, disappointed and relieved at the same time. She'd gotten Johan's thoughts steered in another direction, and yet at the same time she yearned to be snuggling with him.

He lit his pipe and took a couple long drags. Elise marveled at his strong hands. It was strange that a few small movements of those two hands could arouse such wonderful tingly feelings in her body.

"Have you told your mother?"

"No, I don't dare. It'll be the death of her. We'll have to say it's someone else, someone who Hilda can marry after a while."

"Sooner or later you'll have to tell her."

"We can't. I wouldn't wish that shame on anyone, least of all Mamma."

He drew in a deep heavy sigh. "Has Hilda been seeing Lorang, the errand boy, lately?"

"I don't know. I can ask. What are you thinking?"

"I thought… Maybe it might be an idea to talk with him. Slip him a few *kroner* or something…"

"Where would we get those *kroner* from?"

"I'll help you with that."

"You? And where would you get the money from?"

He smiled. "I'll find a second job." He lifted his arm and proudly showed his muscles bulging through his shirt sleeves. "I can heave pallets down at Seilduken after my regular work hours."

She stared at him, wide eyed. "Can you handle that?"

He chuckled. "Haven't you noticed I have more strength than I need?"

Elise blushed, red in her cheeks. Johan had plenty of strength. No doubt about it.

Chapter 17

They stood dressed in black, mute and with heavy thoughts, gathered around the grave at Nordre Gravlund. Now Pappa was in the ground, in a pauper's coffin, covered with many small pine branches. Not as much as one flower for him. It was sad, even if he had been a drunkard and a good for nothing. All deserved a flower on their grave, Elise thought, a soft-hearted sadness filling her chest.

Nearly everyone from the *gård* had come: Fru Evertsen and her sister, Fru Albertsen and old Fru Berg from the neighboring *gård*, the *gård* manager and his wife, Johan and Fru Thoresen, as well as several of the girls from the spinning mill. Dressed in black, many with a pine twig in their hands had followed the *likkjerra* with the black drapery. It had been pulled by a horse covered with a black blanket. After the coffin had been lowered into the ground, the minister said "ashes to ashes, dust to dust...," the grave digger covered it with earth, and the mourners silently laid their pine twigs on it, one by one.

It was so silent and unnatural. No one spoke, no music, no hymns. They couldn't afford a bell-ringer or a choir, and none of them felt an urge to sing a verse of a hymn either.

Suddenly the silence was broken by a deep and melodious man's voice:

"O take my hand, dear Father, and lead Thou me, till at my journey's ending I dwell with Thee. Alone I cannot wander one single day, so do Thou guide my footsteps on life's rough way."

Elise stood motionless and held her breath. It was so beautiful she was afraid of collapsing then and there, she who'd been composed through it all until now. She was spellbound and didn't dare turn to see who sang with such a beautiful voice. She was afraid of breaking the spell, wanted to enjoy it a little longer, without seeing, only feeling. Her breathing was nearly paralyzed when the man started to sing the second verse.

After the last stanza drifted out in the sparkling, cold January day, not a person moved. It was as if the hymn had lifted them up, carried them away on wings to a place high up in the clouds, to a better and different world. A small sob could be heard, some sniffled, some dared to look back, and others didn't.

When the mourners started shaking hands with Elise before wandering back home, she turned her head to the side. She caught a glimpse of a tall, dark figure, moving slowly in the other direction. A Salvation Army officer...

"Who was that?" Johan, by her side, asked curiously.

"I don't know. Probably somebody who sings at funerals."

"How strange it was one of *them*..."

"Is that so strange? They are believers, too, even if they wear uniforms."

Peder was pulling at her black shawl. "Come on, Elise. I'm freezin' cold."

Elise glanced down at him. His eyes were red, and his look so painful she had to glance away. "Ja, let's hurry home to Mamma," she said and took his hand. To her amazement he didn't pull his hand away. Then Johan grabbed his other hand, and he was walking between them.

They walked for a while without talking. Even Johan was quiet. Kristian and Hilda came behind them, with Johan's mother and some others.

Suddenly, Peder, in amazement blurted out, "Did ya hear whad he sang? I can't go alone, he san'. where da other one goes, he shoul' follow after, he said."

"He meant God."

Peder shot a questioning glance up at her. "Was it 'im Pappa should follow?"

Elise nodded.

"Does God wanna go wid' Pappa, den?"

"God loves everyone. It doesn't matter what they do."

"So Pappa ain't alone after all, ya mean?"

"No, now he's not alone."

Peder chuckled, more to himself: "Den I t'ink I'll be happy when it's *my* turn."

Elise had to swallow the lump in her throat, but smiled and sent a quick glance over to Johan. He smiled back.

They'd come almost all the way home. Elise turned around to make sure Hilda was with them. Then she saw Hilda had stopped. Valborg stood and whispered something to her. Immediately when they noticed Elise looking at them, Valborg turned her face away. "I hafta go, see ya later, Hilda."

One of the other girls from the spinning mill came towards Elise to shake her hand. "I couldn't do it at the cemetery," she said. She was shy and unable to make eye contact.

"I must hurry up to Anna," Fru Thoresen said and disappeared through the gate. Then they were all alone. The silence enveloped them like a blanket.

Elise turned to Johan. "Will you come up to the kitchen for a *kaffesvett*?"

He nodded.

When they reached the *gård*, Elise turned to face Hilda. "What did Valborg want with you?"

Hilda shrugged her shoulders.

"She gave me such a dirty look."

"She only thought it kinda strange that your buddy from the Salvation Army came and sang."

Elise felt her face turn red. "My buddy? What kind of nonsense is that?"

"Her girlfriend recognized 'im again."

Johan stopped abruptly and turned toward them with a perplexed facial expression. "Was it the man who walked you home from the Temple?"

"I have no idea who it was." She was getting upset. "I only saw it was a Salvation Army officer."

Johan sputtered. "Dammit."

"Johan, you're swearin'!" Peder gave him an indignant look. "And today when Pappa was buried."

They walked in silence through the entryway and all the steps up to the third floor.

When they came into the kitchen, Elise quickly rekindled the fire, while Hilda went into the *kammers* to see Mamma and tell her about the funeral. Peder and Kristian were loud and excited. It wasn't every day Johan sat with them at the kitchen table.

But Johan was strangely quiet. When spoken to he answered with clipped, short words. When Elise directed her eyes at him, she saw his eyes were locked on following her every move.

He wasn't so dumb that he was bothered by the man from the Salvation Army? The thought irritated her.

Right now she felt vulnerable. She wanted to hold onto the beautiful memory of the song, keep it as a priceless treasure which she could find again when her thoughts drifted to Pappa. Not because it had been *him* - she thought she'd recognized him when she'd gotten a glimpse of him - but because the hymn had been so beautiful and had given a dignified ending to the funeral. The silent mourners, all dressed in black, had surrounded the pauper's grave, with the delicate sparkling frost-laden trees and the clear January sky as the only frame, and suddenly - that beautiful, deep voice broke the silence and had sent shivers through her body.

She poured weak coffee with sugar for all of them and put bread, butter, syrup and a five-*øre* cake for each of them on the table. Hilda took a tray in to Mamma.

"How come we are gettin' so much good stuff?" Peder asked in amazement.

"Because Pappa got buried, you dummy." Kristian sent him a disgruntled look.

"Ya mean we're celebratin'?"

"Ja," Elise said loudly. "We are celebrating because Pappa is walking with God."

Peder smiled, satisfied. "An' he ain't drunk no more."

Again Elise felt a lump of betrayal in her throat, and went to the stove pretending to get the coffee kettle again.

After they'd eaten, her brothers wanted to go sliding on the slope by the bridge near the small wooden frame house, belonging to the foreman.

"Watch out for the river, boys," Elise shouted adamantly after them when they rushed out. Cold shivers rushed through her body. There had been enough accidents this year.

Hilda was still in with Mamma.

Johan peered at her. "What's with this guy, Elise?" Apparently that question had been burning on the tip of his tongue since they'd come up.

Elise took a long deep breath. "Nothing, Johan. I had never seen him before I went to the Temple on Monday. I haven't seen him since and I don't want to see him again, either."

"Why is he chasing after you, then?"

Elise forced herself to stay calm. "He's not chasing after me. He is a Christian, he heard that Pappa had fallen in the river and drowned. He knew we couldn't afford a singer or a bell-ringer, that's why he was there, like a good, caring Salvation Army officer. It wasn't for *me*, it was for Pappa."

"I'm not so sure about *that*," Johan grumbled.

She went over to him and put her arms around his neck. "You know what, Johan? I'm flattered that you are jealous, but you are more handsome when you're not."

He finally warmed up and smiled. "Is it any wonder I'm jealous? I'm engaged to the most beautiful girl in all of Sagene."

Elise laughed and met his kiss with closed eyes.

The *kammers* door opened.

"Elise, Mamma wants you to come in."

Elise went in quietly and moved slowly towards her mother's bed.

Mamma sat propped up on her pillows, with a pale, weak smile on her lips and large, clear eyes. In her lap laid the old, worn out Bible she had inherited from her father, and on the dresser a white candle was burning.

Elise took in the sight of her mother with the flicking candle light and the old Bible in her lap, and knew this was a moment she would cherish for a lifetime.

Her mother stretched out a pale, frail hand, Elise gently took and held it.

"Hilda told me everything. Also about the Salvation Army officer who sang."

Elise nodded. "It was so beautiful. I so wish you had been there."

Mamma smiled. "I was so happy when I heard about it. I laid here and cried because there wouldn't be any hymns sung for him. You know, he was a good person. Before the moonshine took control of him."

Elise nodded but said nothing, cherishing the moment, happy to see that Mamma looked better and had been able to share what she had on her heart.

"You must tell the boys when they are older." Mamma was so eager that she became short winded. Elise hoped she hadn't over-exerted and would be worse. "Make them understand their father wasn't always the way they remember him," she continued in a strained voice. "Tell them he was the best looking and fittest man in the whole area of Sagene, that he had a beautiful voice and he was a brave sailor. Just like in the poem *The Norwegian Sailor* written by Bjørnstjerne Bjørnson ..." Her voice faltered, and she closed her eyes and sank back.

Elise stroked her hand caringly over Mamma's cheek. "I'll tell them, Mamma. All that you've told me, I will share with them when they're old enough to understand."

She went quietly back to the kitchen. As she opened the door, she caught a glimpse of Hilda disappearing and slamming the door hard behind her.

Elise looked over at Johan, stunned. "What's with her?"

"I let her understand that I know and told her to quit roaming around at night. It's not right that *you* have to carry the load all alone here."

Elise looked at him in disbelief! "Did you say that I'd told you about the *verksmester*? She'll never forgive me. I promised I wouldn't tell anyone. Now maybe she won't ever come home again."

"Sooner or later I would have heard it, Elise. No one can keep stuff like that to themselves."

Elise sighed in exasperation, "You don't understand, Johan. Hilda is not like your sister. When she's really angry, you never know what she'll do."

Johan got up from the stool and came over to her. "Don't take it so hard. I only wanted to help you." He put his arms around her and pulled her close to him.

She pushed him away. "I think it's better that you leave, Johan. I need to be alone for a while. I have after all followed my father to his grave today...."

He nodded, disappointed, but too proud to protest.

Elise stood and watched him leave. For a brief second, she wanted to run after him, throw her arms around his neck and beg him to come back, but she stood motionless.

Deep in thought she started peeling potatoes. Her red and cracked fingers ached in the icy cold water. Nevertheless suddenly a man's voice resonated in her ears with his deep and beautiful voice: "O take my hand, dear Father, and lead Thou me...."

She pushed the singing voice and the pleasant memory aside. "My buddy, what a thing to say," she sputtered into the wash pan and attacked the potato so hard that the knife slipped and cut her finger.

Evening came; her brothers were getting ready for bed, red cheeks after sledding, wet to the skin and freezing cold, a new luster in their eyes. Hilda still hadn't come back.

"Where's Hilda?" came from Mamma, her voice was weak and worried.

"I think she needed some time alone," Elise answered, evasively. "It's been a heavy day."

Mamma was quiet, so Elise quickly broke the silence, "You've probably heard she has a new girlfriend. She's from a *husmannsplass* by Lake Mjøsa and moved here to town when she was only fifteen years old. Now she's renting a little attic room in the old house down by Seilduken."

She was quiet a few seconds, then from her dark corner in the *kammers* Mamma said, "I hope she's a decent girl."

"I'm sure she is," Elise answered quickly.

But when the boys were in bed, Mamma was settled for the night and she sat alone in the kitchen, fear, doubt and anxiety returned!

Chapter 18

Elise saw no sign of Hilda when she got up the next morning, either. She hadn't been in her bed, wasn't sitting in the kitchen and there were no signs that she'd been there.

Mamma was sleeping, thankfully, so she didn't have to make up a lie. Every now and then the fear popped up again, the same paralyzing fear she'd had that morning when she'd thought it was Hilda laying stiff and frozen down by the bridge. But she succeeded in chasing it away. When Hilda had been so delighted with her new life - cakes and chocolates and a "dirty" old-man who liked to fondle her body - she wouldn't do anything hazardous. In any case, not yet. Not as long as she didn't show and she didn't have to tell the other girls who the father was. Hilda would never tell - the *verksmester* would forbid it.

No, she was more than likely fuming because Elise had talked behind her back to Johan and was punishing her by staying away all night.

"Hey, Hilda wadn't in bed last nite."

Elise was startled and turned abruptly to Peder. "You don't have to say it so loud that Mamma hears it."

"Everybody in the street knows already," Kristian said sarcastically.

"What does everybody know?" Elise looked straight into his eyes.

"That she's out runnin' around, both day 'n nite."

Elise bit her lips and put bread out on the table. As long as they didn't know who Hilda was with, probably she could relax, she thought.

Peder looked sincerely at her. "I'm so glad you 'ave Johan, Elise. So you don' need to go furt'er 'an down the steps."

She smiled at him. "When we get married, I can run up here both morning and night, make something to eat and stuff like that."

Peder looked at her, panic in his face, "Elise, you ain't getting' married for a long time, are ya?"

Elise ran her fingers quickly over a briskly clump of his hair, "Oh no, Peder. Not for a while."

He smiled, evidently relieved.

"I've got to run, the factory siren is howling."

She bundled the thick, prickly shawl extra tight around her head and shoulders. The kitchen was ice cold this morning, so it had to be even much colder outside. "Don't forget to give Mamma some coffee and food before you go to school."

"*Nei da*, stop nagging," Kristian grunted.

"I won't forget, Elise." Peder waved as she went out the door.

She had hoped to run into Johan on her way out, but didn't see anything of him. Oh, I hope that he's not mad at me. Her thoughts were heavy, but she hurried on her way. It was the first time she had pushed him away, the first time she'd torn herself from his arms without needing to because someone was coming. She had even told him to leave. Not all guys would accept their girlfriends treating them that way. She knew that.

But, then Johan wasn't like all the other guys either. He was mature and sensible. He would understand.

When she'd come way down to the bridge she saw some youngsters in the light under the gas street lamp. They were arguing about something or the other, and in an instant they started attacking each other in full-fledged fist fights.

She stopped abruptly, even though the factory sirens had blown long ago. "Stop it kids! Don't you have anything better to do so early in the morning than fight?"

They stopped immediately and gawked at her. Then she noticed one of them was Evert.

"Evert, why are *you* up so early? The store doesn't open for a long time."

He didn't answer, just stood kicking with the toe of his overshoe at an ice-clump.

Elise was about to hurry along, when she heard one of the other boys whisper to another, "Was it *'er* fiancé who dunnit?"

It was as if a pang shot through her. Had Evert spread rumors anyway? Even though she had given him money to keep his mouth shut?

She forced herself to run along, telling herself she hadn't heard anything. After she'd gone a ways, she heard another harsh shout, "Daaaamn, he musta hit him real hard. Imagine fallin' in!"

Elise felt pressure building up around her. If the police were tipped off that Johan had been in a fist fight with Pappa just before he fell in the river, he could be called in. Suspected of manslaughter.

It was urgent she take another trip to Evert tonight. Force him to tell the boys he'd had only made it up. She'd have to give him half of her week's wages and they'd eat *velling* every day.

The next moment she calmed down. The police had other things to do than listen to rambunctious kids telling cops and robbers stories. They wouldn't even bother to listen to them. At least not to snotty brats like Evert, homeless and supported by the Poor House. Besides, Evert had too much fear for Hermansen's wrath to let it out that he'd been gone all night.

To her relief she spotted Hilda immediately as she came into the spinning mill. She was chattering away with Valborg and some others, giggling and laughing, smiling and putting on airs. The girls flocked around her. But she didn't send as much as a glance in Elise's direction.

That didn't matter, thankfully she was alive, Elise sighed.

At the same time she felt ashamed. She was furious with Evert for blabbering but she had done exactly the same. It was true, though, there was a big difference --- she had done it in hopes of getting good advice from Johan, but Evert had only done it to have shocking gossip to tell the other boys. But, seen from the outside, maybe there wasn't such a huge difference after all. Neither of them had kept their promise.

Finally it was lunch time, the machines stopped and lunch buckets were heard rattling out in the hallway.

Elise glanced over at Hilda to see if she gave any sign of going home, but she was surrounded by the other bobbin girls, chatting, waving her arms and laughing. There was no indication she was planning to leave the spinning mill soon.

Maybe Johan will come home today for lunch, Elise thought hopefully when she walked briskly, shivering, over the bridge. It had been so special the last time he'd run home during the lunch break to be with her. "We have nothing to complain about, we who have each other," he had said. He was right. One can tolerate a lot in this life, when you're so blessed to have one you love.

It wasn't worth it to tell him what Evert and his buddies had talked about. It would just upset him. If Evert refused to go along with her, she'd threaten him that Johan would come and set him straight. That should scare him. The boys in the street had respect for Johan.

She hoped the slum-sister wasn't there right now. It wasn't that she didn't want her to visit. Quite the opposite, she was so thankful that Mamma was getting help. Hilda had gotten new boots and they'd also gotten a whole loaf of bread. But the slum-sister would perhaps look down on her if she had a gentleman caller and it would ruin the chance for her and Johan to have a few minutes alone.

She wanted desperately to fix things with Johan again. If he came home during the lunch break she would throw her arms around him and show him how much she loved him, until they'd have to rush off to work again. She would tell him about the twinges of guilt she'd felt after he'd left last night and how she'd wanted to erase what she'd said and be in his arms all night.

It was quiet in the *gård*. Those not working were either huddled up in their kitchens trying to find warmth from the freezing winter cold or hanging around one of all the beer-joints down at Vaterland. The women were at Hjula Weaving Mill or Nedre Vøien Spinning Mill.

Mamma and Anna laid alone, each on separate floors. It would have been so much better if they could keep each other company. A spasm of guilt struck her when she thought about Anna. She had promised to visit soon, but hadn't had time. She could do it now before she went up to Mamma.

She knocked on the door, but there was no answer. So Johan hadn't come home for the lunch break, as she had hoped. The disappointment stung!

She'd hastened her steps all the way home - but he had much further to go. He could still come.

The door was never locked. Why should it be? There wasn't much to steal in the Andersengård. She carefully opened the door and went in.

The little kitchen was clean and tidy, as always. Fru Thoresen was a work-horse. It was hard to comprehend that she was able to do so much. On top of that, she was often forced to work overtime with no extra pay. On the wobbly old kitchen table lay a small, clean and freshly ironed tablecloth, the kerosene lamp was polished and the floor by the woodstove was swept clean of the dust and dirt brought in with the firewood.

She went over to the *kammers* door and knocked gently.

"Come in." Anna's voice was soft and weak.

Elise tip-toed in quietly, like when one sneaks into a *kammers* where someone's sleeping.

"Elise?" Anna's pale face lit up when she saw her. "Are you coming to visit me?" She lifted her head up from the pillow, her dark hair hanging lightly on her shoulders, her blue eyes wide and framed with thick, black eyelashes. If Anna had been like other girls, the boys would be flocking around her, Elise thought.

"I have to go and take care of Mamma, but wanted to say hello to you first."

"You are the kindest person I know. Well, next to my brother," Anna giggled.

"He comes home during the lunch-break sometimes, doesn't he?"

"Yes, but not today. He had something he had to take care of."

Elise swallowed her disappointment.

"He told me about the funeral. I so wanted to be there, Elise. For your sake."

Elise wondered if he'd also told her about the Salvation Army officer, but didn't say it out loud.

"Tell me how you have been," she continued. "What's happening at the spinning mill, how's it going with Hilda?

Johan hinted there are some problems, but wouldn't say what."

Elise avoided Anna's questioning eyes. She would like to confide in Anna, but couldn't. It was bad enough that Johan knew. Even if sooner or later it would be known, it was still awhile before she would show. "She's not home much nowadays..." she started.

Anna smiled. "It's Lorang, isn't it?"

Elise's eyes shifted again avoiding eye contact. "Peder says he's seen them together," she mumbled.

"Did you know that Lorang used to drop by to see me often last summer?"

Elise was taken by surprise. "No, I didn't know that."

"Mamma didn't like it. She says I have to be content with my fate. But, when I am laying here alone I often dream I am just like the rest of you and I am going steady with Lorang. He was so kind. He read to me, brought me daisies and sometimes he brought old women's magazines he had gotten from Magda on the Corner. I saved them for a long time, but Mamma needed to burn them in the stove when we were short of firewood. "They had such beautiful pictures," she fantasized. "Beautiful women wearing silk and velvet, men and women walking arm in arm in a park full of colorful flowers and young girls in white, elegant dresses with parasols and hats with veils..."

She shook her head, as if wanting to shake the beautiful pictures and memories from her mind. She looked up at Elise with a playful smile on her colorless lips. "I know very well why you never noticed that Lorang was here. It was the same time that Johan and you became sweethearts..."

Elise blushed. In a flashback, she saw herself and Johan up in the meadow again, without a care or a thought in the world, other than being together.

Anna became serious again. "Johan is so much in love with you, Elise. Excuse me for asking, but did something happen yesterday? I mean… I know it was a hard day for all of you, but was there something else? Is there something between you and Johan?"

A sharp bolt of pain shot through Elise. Had Johan been so upset that Anna had noticed? She shook her head. "It was just that I was tired. I was so exhausted and worn out I didn't know what to do with myself."

"I understand. You've got so much - the job at the spinning mill, your mother, and Peder and Kristian."

"Why do you ask? Did Johan say something?"

"No, I just noticed there seemed something heavy on his mind. At first I thought it was something about the funeral, but…" Anna shrugged and dropped her shoulders. "I have no idea what it was."

"Is there something I can help you with? If Johan isn't coming home during the lunch break, it'll be a very long day for you to wait until your mother and he are back from the factories."

"If you could help me up to the chamber pot and then grab the blanket off Johan's bed and put it over me. I've been laying here freezing ever since last night. I really wish there were nothing called winter," she shuddered.

Elise did as Anna requested. Then asked, "Aren't you hungry?"

"There's food under the cover on the tinplate over there." Elise brought it to her.

"I think I'll go up to Mamma now. I can rather come down an evening soon and read a little to you again, Anna."

Anna smiled. "No wonder Johan loves you."

When Elise came into their own kitchen, she saw immediately that someone had been there. A loaf of bread was on the table and the coffee kettle was warm. She opened the door to the *kammers*.

Mamma was sitting up in bed, supported by pillows, her hair freshly combed and she was wearing a clean, ironed nightgown.

"Has the slum sister been here?"

Mamma nodded, smiling. "She brought hot vegetable soup, with meat, for me. She is so kind, Elise. I just don't know how she does it. One of the other slum sisters was infected and has gotten tuberculosis. They work themselves to death."

She stretched her arm to Elise, as she sat down on the edge of the bed taking Mamma's thin hand in hers. Before she'd thought it was painful to see Mamma's hands red, cracked and frost-bitten, but now it was even worse to see them so thin and white, her blood veins looking like rivers on an old map.

"I'm so glad you went to the Temple and got us some help," she continued. "Did you know that it was the Salvation Army officer who walked you home who came and sang at the gravesite?"

"One of the factory girls told me. I only saw that it was one of them."

"His name is Emanuel Ringstad and he is a captain. They become captains after Officer's Training School and five years of service. He was only nineteen years old when he joined the Salvation Army and has been part of it since. Maren Sørby, the slum sister, spoke very highly of him. She said he does more than most, not just with the evangelical part, but with also the social problems. He often goes to the cemetery and sings at funerals for poor folks. He knows they don't have money for a choir."

That's something for Johan to hear, Elise thought. It wasn't because of her that he'd come, he frequently sings at funerals. She would tell Johan when he came home this evening.

"Next time you go to the Temple, you must thank him from me. Say I was so pleased. Tell him that is the most beautiful hymn I know."

Elise nodded. "I think you look a little better today, Mamma."

Her mother gave her a weak, little smile. "You see there is hope for me after all. Thanks to you, Elise."

In the next second she was serious again. "There's one thing I've been thinking I want to ask you. Please tell me about your problems. It's much worse to lay here and imagine things, catch a word here and a word there, and understand that there's something you won't say to me, than to hear the truth."

She stopped, had to catch her breath. It'd been a long time since Mamma had said so much at one time.

"I understand you don't want to burden me, but think if it were you. Would you want to be kept out of it if you understood something serious was going on with your loved ones?"

Elise fidgeted. She couldn't tell her, but at the same time she couldn't lie to Mamma.

"I can see that you're hurting, Elise. I suspect you promised not to say anything. Then I'll help you. Is Hilda pregnant?"

Elise dropped Mamma's hand, gazed down at her lap, twisting her fingers nervously.

Mamma gave a heavy sigh. "It won't be worse for us than for others…..."

There was silence between them a short while.

"If only she gets to keep her job, we'll get along."

Mamma sighed deeply again. "There is The Crib….." She leaned her head back and closed her eyes, then opened them again. "As long as he isn't out of work, he should certainly be able to help a little. I mean the man she's in love with."

Elise's mouth was dry, words would not come.

Mamma clutched her hand. "I'll talk with Hilda, Elise. It wasn't fair of me to pressure you. You two have always been good friends, so I thought…I thought it would be easier for her to confide in a sister than to her old mother."

"You are not old, Mamma," Elise protested, thinking she had to make Hilda wait with telling the entire truth. It could be too much for Mamma.

"How's Johan doing?"

Elise felt Mamma's eyes scrutinizing her. Had she overheard what she and Johan had talked about in the kitchen after they came home from the funeral? She couldn't remember if they had exchanged harsh words. "He's just fine. I thought maybe he would come home for lunch today, but Anna told me he had some errands to run."

"Have you been down with Anna?"

"I stopped in on my way up. She is always so happy and grateful. I don't understand how she does it." Elise stood up from the edge of the bed. "But, now I have to go to the kitchen and cook up some *velling*. Peder and Kristian need something to eat when they come home from school."

"The slum sister was so talkative. She told things that scared me."

Elise stopped. "Scared you?"

"She told me they are expecting an epidemic of smallpox and folks are flocking to the doctor to get vaccinated."

Elise furrowed her brow. It really hadn't been necessary to frighten her mother with such information, Elise thought.

"And then she told me it's beginning to get even harder for folks. The business people are calling it "the crash." More and more folks are losing their jobs and poverty is growing. Every day there are longer and longer lines in front of the soup kitchens. She told me it wasn't just the old folks and mothers with small children standing in the lines, but young girls and strong, young men, as well. All of them not working."

Elise nodded. This wasn't anything new. At the same time, she was surprised at her mother's eagerness to tell about it. She was grateful to see that Mamma felt better, and now understood how alone Mamma felt since she tried to keep her as long as possible. She stood beside her, didn't have the heart to leave her quite yet.

"She talked on and on and said it looks like the Norway-Sweden union will be dissolved."

Elise nodded. "Agnes has told me that, her father knows what's happening. And Johan keeps talking about it, too."

"It frightens me. The slum sister said this could mean war with Sweden."

"That's not for sure, Mamma. Even if a war breaks out, it's not sure *we'll* notice it that much. Agnes' father doesn't think it'll make any difference if Norway becomes free or not. Not for us workers, at least."

Her mother sank back in the pillows again and closed her eyes. "There is too much to worry about. I don't think I want to think about it now."

"Get some sleep, Mamma. I'm going to the kitchen and put wood in the stove."

When Elise, a little later, wrapped the gray knit shawl tightly around her head and shoulders and hurried out in the winter cold again, she decided to walk home from the spinning mill with Hilda this evening. She would tell her what Mamma had said and at the same time beg her earnestly not to reveal more than necessary. As long as their mother believed that Hilda had fallen in love with a boy and gotten pregnant, she could handle it. But knowing that Hilda had gone to bed with that old man... She gritted her teeth and walked even faster.

Johan's suggestion tumbled around in her head. Maybe Lorang would agree to it? It looked like he cared for Hilda. At least he had earlier this winter, long after he'd visited Anna. He only had to pretend he was the father of the baby. That would be that! That the *verksmester* helped out with a few *kroner* and "took care of it" was only fair and reasonable. No, maybe Johan's suggestion wasn't a bad idea. It would save Mamma and all of them from shame.

The first she did when she came back to the spinning mill was look for Hilda. Luckily she was in her place. She wasn't quite sure what she'd feared, but Hilda did so many stupid things these days, you never know.

The rest of the day was just as long and hard as usual and maybe even longer. She was impatient, wanting to talk with Hilda.

When the factory siren finally blew, she kept a steady eye on Hilda not wanting to lose sight of her on the way out. Hilda walked with several other girls, Elise had to wait until they'd crossed over the bridge and the others disappeared.

Finally when they were close to Andersengård, they were alone.

"Hilda, I have to talk with you."

Hilda turned abruptly. Elise couldn't see her face, but felt Hilda's unforgiving scowl. "I'm never telling *you* anything again!"

"Mamma has figured it out."

She saw Hilda's body stiffen. "Did you blabber to her, too?!" Her voice was angry.

"No, it was her; she came right out and asked me." She grabbed Hilda's arm. "You absolutely *can not* tell her who it is!"

Hilda pulled away, ran through the entryway and hurried up the steps, Elise right behind her.

As she came up to the second floor she heard the sounds of agitated, angry voices and scuffling of feet from Johan's kitchen. Just them the door opened and Johan came out, followed by two constables.

His face was ashen gray, and when he recognized it was her, he sent her an anguished glance. "I have to go to the police station, Elise."

Elise panicked. She had a feeling that her heart had stopped beating. "What is it?" Her voice so weak it came out in a whisper.

The constables jabbed and shoved Johan and sent her a dark warning glance. Evert has squealed - she thought in dispair.

So it was Johan who'd killed Pappa after all...

Glossary

Much has been written about Norwegians who emigrated from Norway during the mass exodus in 1865-1930 when more than 780,000 emigrated from Norway to America. The population had grown in such large numbers that it was not possible to live and survive in rural Norway.

But what happened to the hundreds of folk who did not, could not, would not leave Norway? Many moved to industrial areas in hopes of finding work in factories.They experienced a completely foreign life, too, compared to the rural life they'd known.

Those immigrating to America and those migrating into Kristiania brought with them the same Norwegian language and many of the same words and expressions. Therefore, in this translation a glossary is included because occasionally it is necessary to use Norwegian words in the text to capture the spirit, the mood, and the feeling.

Akerselva – a large river, with many waterfalls, running through Kristiania (Oslo). It generated water power for several large factories which needed workers. An *elv* is a river.

Åsgårdsreia – Superstitious belief that ghosts of the dead suddenly returned. The ghosts flew through the air on horses to take the living between December 13 and Christmas Eve. The sign of the cross on the door would save folks from being taken by the ghosts.

busserull – distinctive style of typical work and everyday shirt worn by factory workers and farmers. In the last 130–

180 years the Norwegian *busserull* has been made of one–
color, checked or striped fabric of wool or cotton, from the
neck band to the chest there is a split with a couple of buttons.
(See Johan on the cover.)

Christiania Brœndevinssamlag – an alcohol distillery in
Kristiania which donated from their profits to worthy
organizations and causes.

En Glad Gutt – *A Happy Boy* written by Bjørnstein Bjørnsen.

fleskebiter – pieces of pork, salted and smoked, similar but
thicker than bacon.

Fru – title for either a married woman or a widow; Mrs.

Fy! – expression for something shameful.

gård – a tenement building with backyard in a city or town; a
farm in the rural area.

grøt – cooked milk, flour wisped in until thick, little salt is
added. Eaten warm. Type of porridge or mush.

Herberget – rooming house of meager standard.

Herr – title for an adult male; Mr.

husmannsplass – A *husmann* was a farm laborer, tenant
farmer or hired man, who received a minimum wage, small
house and farm buildings, with or without a small patch of
land for his own use in return for working for a farmer with a

larger amount of land. Therefore, his place was called a *husmannsplass*.

Ja – Yes, both formal and informal.

kaffeskvett – a drop of coffee.

kammers – most homes had only 2 rooms, a kitchen and a *kammers*. The *kammers* functioned as both the sleeping room and living room. Some homes had only the *kammers* and a shared kitchen with one or several families.

kirke – church.

kjerring – slang for a woman, wife, or an older woman, often has a negative undertone. *Kjerringene* - plural form of *kjerring*.

kremmerhus – a triangular cone shaped bag, formed by folding paper at right angles.

Kristiania – the official name for Oslo from 1624 to 1925.

krone – money. The value of one krone in 1905 was approximately 27 cents. One dollar was worth approximately 3.73 kroner. K*roner* - the form plural.

likkjerra – horse drawn wagon that carried the funeral wooden box (casket).

odelsgutt – oldest son with legal right to inherit the farm.

natta, natta – good night or "nighty, night."

n*ei da!* – no.

nisser – small supernatural beings who are cousins to gnomes, said to live underground. Wear red stocking caps.

S*agene* – Section of Kristiania.

Nordre Gravlund – gravlund is a graveyard/cemetery; the North Cemetery in Kristiania.

sild – herring; poor man's food in 1905.

skaut – kerchief; woman's head scarf, a square woolen or cotton cloth folded over in triangular shape and tied under the chin.

skyggelua – a flat cap, somewhat floppy, with a visor. Could also be called six–pence. (See picture of Johan on cover).

s*kål* – "cheers."

St. Hansaften – Norwegian name for Midsummer Night, which is June 23rd.

takk; tusen takk – thank you; thousand thanks.

The Frog – nickname given to the foreman by the spinning girls and bobbin girls who worked in the spinning mill.

velling – a thin porridge or gruel of boiled milk or water thickened with barley flour, until slightly thick. Very nutritious.

verksmester – the supervisor at Nedre Vøien Spinderi.

Øre – money. 1\100 of 1 krone. 10 øre in 1905 was worth
approximately 3 cents

The actual names of most streets, bridges, churches and
places have not been translated. Most names are the same
today as they were in 1905, i.e. Akersbakken, Sandakerveien,
Mariadalsveien, Seilduksgata, Østgaardsgate and several
others. (Names ending with *veien* and *gate (a)* are street
names.) Beirerbrua is the name of the bridge over Akerselva.
(Bru (a) means bridge.)

CPSIA information can be obtained at www.ICGtesting.com
Printed in the USA
BVOW07s0951120913

331014BV00001B/1/P